"I want to kiss you

Annie's heart leapt.

"But I won't if you don't want me to.

In answer, she leaned toward him and whispered, "I do."

And then she was in his arms. His mouth lowered to hers. One kiss became two, three. The only reality for Annie was Kevin, and the way he made her feel.

But when Kevin came up for air, Annie suddenly came back down to earth, and a feeling of panic set in. Abruptly she put her hands on his chest and pushed away. "I'm—I'm sorry. I can't."

Slowly she raised her eyes, and what she saw in his calmed her. He wasn't angry. So why was she so scared? "I'm—I'm just not ready."

"I know, and it's okay. I'm a patient man." Kevin's smile was tender. "But when you *are* ready, I'll be waiting."

Dear Reader,

Our resolution is to start the year with a bang in Silhouette Special Edition! And so we are featuring Peggy Webb's *The Accidental Princess*—our pick for this month's READERS' RING title. You'll want to use the riches in this romance to facilitate discussions with your friends and family! In this lively tale, a plain Jane agrees to be the local Dairy Princess and wins the heart of the bad-boy reporter who wants her story…among other things.

Next up, Sherryl Woods thrills her readers once again with the newest installment of THE DEVANEYS—*Michael's Discovery*. Follow this ex-navy SEAL hero as he struggles to heal from battle—and save himself from falling hard for his beautiful physical therapist! Pamela Toth's *Man Behind the Badge,* the third book in her popular WINCHESTER BRIDES miniseries, brings us another stunning hero in the form of a flirtatious sheriff, whose wild ways are numbered when he meets—and wants to rescue—a sweet, yet reclusive woman with a secret past. Talking about secrets, a doctor hero is stunned when he finds a baby— maybe even *his* baby—on the doorstep in Victoria Pade's *Maybe My Baby,* the second book in her BABY TIMES THREE miniseries. Add a feisty heroine to the mix, and you have an instant family.

Teresa Southwick delivers an unforgettable story in *Midnight, Moonlight & Miracles*. In it, a nurse feels a strong attraction to her handsome patient, yet she doesn't want him to discover the *real* connection between them. And Patricia Kay's *Annie and the Confirmed Bachelor* explores the blossoming love between a self-made millionaire and a woman who can't remember her past. Can their romance survive?

This month's lineup is packed with intrigue, passion, complex heroines and heroes who never give up. Keep your own resolution to live life romantically, with a treat from Silhouette Special Edition. Happy New Year, and happy reading!

Karen Taylor Richman
Senior Editor

Please address questions and book requests to:
Silhouette Reader Service
U.S.: 3010 Walden Ave., P.O. Box 1325, Buffalo, NY 14269
Canadian: P.O. Box 609, Fort Erie, Ont. L2A 5X3

Annie and the Confirmed Bachelor

PATRICIA KAY

SPECIAL EDITION™

Published by Silhouette Books

America's Publisher of Contemporary Romance

For my wonderful Circle of Sisters:
Allison Leigh, Cheryl Reavis, Lisette Belisle,
Christine Flynn, Myrna Temte, Lois Dyer,
Laurie Campbell and Julia Mozingo.

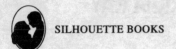 SILHOUETTE BOOKS

ISBN 0-373-24518-1

ANNIE AND THE CONFIRMED BACHELOR

Copyright © 2003 by Patricia A. Kay

Visit Silhouette at www.eHarlequin.com

Printed in U.S.A.

Chapter One

Annie Alcott pulled into the driveway of the small apartment complex she'd lived in for the past four days. She smiled as she looked at the neat, red brick units bordered by well-tended flower beds.

Country Garden Apartments.

She loved the name. The complex wasn't really in the country, although it was located on the outskirts of Pollero, a small town about forty miles west of Austin, and so far, at least, suburbia hadn't caught up. Behind the complex was dense acreage owned by the county and earmarked for a public park, and everywhere else the eye could see was undeveloped land. Right now, late March, the surrounding hills were covered with wildflowers, predominantly the bluebonnets for which this part of Texas was famous, although today, because of the rain, they were a watery periwinkle blur.

Annie had chosen the apartments not only for the location, which she felt was far enough off the beaten track to escape attention, but because they were so charming with their shuttered windows, white picket fences, gas lights, and brick walkways.

Yet, as attractive as the complex was, an hour after moving in she wondered if she'd made a mistake. No matter how charming, she'd had to give up everything familiar, and she wondered if she would ever get used to practically living as a fugitive.

But those feelings didn't last long, because it was such a blessed relief not to have to worry that any minute Jonathan would show up on her doorstep or call her on the phone.

Now that everything was unpacked and put away and she was beginning to get familiar with Pollero, the apartment had begun to feel like home. She had finally relaxed. Finally begun to think Jonathan wouldn't come after her. Finally begun to believe that maybe, just maybe, he had accepted the divorce.

Please, God…it's nearly a year…

The unfinished prayer had been her litany ever since she'd mustered the courage to leave him. When she'd first moved out of their showplace home—like her, another of Jonathan's trophies—she'd rented an apartment in Austin, near her old stomping grounds, so she could stay close to her friends.

But a month ago she'd finally had to face the fact she would never be free of Jonathan unless she removed herself from his physical sphere. As long as she was close by, he would not leave her alone. He continued to drop by unannounced, continued to harass her via the telephone, and he had even begun to follow her in the evenings and on weekends. When his harassment had extended to the office where she was working, she'd known something had to change.

So she'd moved. She'd purposely chosen a day when she knew he would be in surgery until at least six that evening. And it had worked. She'd escaped, and so far, so good. Of course, in the process, she'd had to give up a job she really liked—the first job she'd had in ten years—and cut all ties, because she knew Jonathan: if any of her friends knew where she'd gone, eventually he would know, too.

She parked the used Toyota she'd purchased to replace her Lexus as close to her back door as she could manage.

She eyed the rain. It was coming down in torrents. She didn't relish getting soaked. Deciding she would wait for the rain to let up a bit, she pulled her cell phone out of her purse and punched in the code for the nursing home in Boston where her great-aunt lived.

"Aunt Deena?" she said when her great-aunt's shaky voice answered.

"Annie? Is it you?"

"Yes, Aunt Deena, it's me."

"Oh, I'm glad. I was beginning to worry."

"I told you I wouldn't call until today."

"I know, but I get nervous when I can't get in touch with you."

"But Aunt Deena…" Annie told herself not to get impatient with her great-aunt. After all, her mother's aunt was ninety-five years old. She forgot things. "I gave you my cell phone number. You know you can call me on it anytime."

"I just don't hold with those fancy newfangled things. I don't trust 'em." This was said in a much firmer tone.

Annie couldn't help it. She chuckled. "I understand, but it isn't as if *you* have to use a cell phone."

"It doesn't matter," her great-aunt said stubbornly. "It's the principle of the thing."

Annie knew better than to argue with the older woman. It would be a losing battle. Her great-aunt had set ideas about things, and no one, not even Annie, would ever change them. "Well, anyway, I've settled into my new apartment and I just wanted to let you know everything is fine."

When her great-aunt didn't respond, Annie said, "Aunt Deena? Did you hear me?"

"Yes, I heard you. I just think it's a terrible shame the way marriages don't seem to last anymore. Why, your great-uncle Harold and I were together for nearly sixty years. It wasn't like we didn't have our ups and downs, either, but we stuck it out. For better or for worse, that's what you youngsters don't seem to realize. I told your mother she was setting a bad example for you and Emily, but would she listen?''

Annie smothered a sigh. She had heard this refrain before. She even agreed with her great-aunt, especially where her mother was concerned. If only she could explain to Aunt Deena. But how could she? She didn't want to upset the older woman, and she knew if she told her the truth about Jonathan, Aunt Deena would be terribly upset, and then she'd worry even more.

''I know,'' she murmured when her great-aunt finally wound down, ''I know. But what's done is done. I'm divorced and I'm trying to build a new life.'' She made her voice upbeat and cheery. ''So. How have you been feeling this week, Aunt Deena?''

''Oh, my rheumatism is giving me trouble, and my eyes just aren't what they used to be, but other than that, I'm fit as a fiddle.''

Annie smiled. *Fit as a fiddle*. That was her aunt's favorite expression. ''That's wonderful.''

''Well, Annie, thank you for calling. But I have to go now. They're ringing the bell for lunch.''

''You don't want to be late for lunch.''

"No, no, I don't. On Thursdays they have meat loaf."

"This is Friday, Aunt Deena," Annie said gently.

"Is it? Oh, dear. I can't remember what they have on Fridays." She sounded as if she were going to cry.

"They have macaroni and cheese on Fridays. Don't they? And fish. You like fish."

"Yes, yes, I do," her aunt said happily. "I *love* fish. Especially when they have that good tartar sauce. Annie, will you tell them to have that tartar sauce?"

"Sure, Aunt Deena. I'll tell them."

"Oh, good. Now. When am I going to see you again?"

"I'm coming for your birthday in June."

"Am I going to have a party?"

"Of course. It isn't every day a woman turns ninety-six."

"And will there be a cake and presents and candles?"

"What's a party without a cake and presents and candles?"

"Yes, you're right. Oh, it will be so much fun. Well, dear, the bell is ringing again. I have to go now. Goodbye."

"Goodbye, Aunt Deena. I'll call you again next Friday."

Annie disconnected the call. Each time they said goodbye she felt sad. Her great-aunt had always been so vibrant; her mind had been so sharp. And now…now instead of guiding Annie and listening to her fears and problems and dreams the way she had when Annie was growing up, their roles had reversed, and it was as if Annie was the adult and her great-aunt was the child.

Sometimes Annie felt so alone. Sure, she had a mother and sister, but her mother lived in London with her third husband, and Emily at forty-two was ten years older than Annie. She and her husband were archaeologists; they traveled constantly. She and Annie had never been close. In fact, it had been three years since they'd seen each other, six months since they'd even talked on the phone.

No wonder I was such easy pickings for Jonathan.

Lost in her pensive thoughts, it took Annie a few minutes to realize the rain wasn't coming down nearly as hard as it had been. It was time to make a run for it. She shoved her cell phone back into her purse.

Then, juggling the purse, her bag of groceries, and her umbrella, she maneuvered herself out of the car and dashed to her back gate.

It took some doing to unlock the back door without getting drenched, but she managed it. Dumping her groceries and purse on the kitchen table, she propped the wet umbrella in the corner and was just unbuttoning her raincoat when the front doorbell rang.

Thinking it was the phone company—she'd requested a jack to be installed in the bedroom and they'd promised to come this afternoon—she hurried through the living room to the front door. So she was totally unprepared to see Jonathan's face through the peephole. Her heart knocked against her chest.

Oh, God, no. No!

She backed away from the door, her mind racing. She wouldn't open it. She didn't care how many times he rang the doorbell or banged on the door, she wasn't going to open it. Eventually he'd get tired and go away.

Or would he?

She remembered how, when one of the surgical nurses had questioned an order he'd given, he had hounded the nurse until she asked for a transfer. She remembered how he'd refused to leave a jewelry shop that had closed five minutes early until they finally reopened the door and waited on him. She remembered how single-minded and relentless he was about anything he wanted.

The doorbell rang again.

She eyed the door. She had the chain on. Maybe if she opened it enough so that they could talk, he would be satisfied.

He can't hurt you if you don't let him in.

Annie took a deep breath. She unlocked the dead bolt and opened the door as wide as the chain would allow.

"Hello, Annie." He gave her one of his boyish, endearing smiles.

"Hello, Jonathan. What are you doing here?" Her voice contained no warmth.

"Ah, come on, Annie. Don't be like that. I just wanted to see you. I have to talk to you."

"We have nothing to talk about. It's all been said." *Over and over again.*

"Annie, I know you're hurt and angry, and I don't blame you. Really I don't. But surely you're not so angry that you won't even listen to me."

She shook her head sadly. "I have listened, Jonathan." *And nothing's changed. Nothing will ever change.* "I don't want to listen anymore."

"Please. Just let me come in. Just long enough to say my piece and afterward, if you want me to, I'll leave. I promise." When she didn't move, he added, "C'mon, have a heart. I'm getting soaked."

"Jonathan…"

"Please, Annie? Please? I promise. I won't stay long. I just want to talk to you for a few minutes."

Oh, God. How did he always manage to make her feel as if she was the one being unreasonable?

"Annie?"

She sighed. She knew him. He wasn't going to go away. He would stand out there all night if he had to, and in the end she'd finally give in. "All right. But just for a few minutes." She closed the door so she could unlatch the chain, then opened it.

As soon as he stepped inside, he tried to take her into his arms, but she shook her head and backed away. "Jonathan, you said you just wanted to talk."

"I know. And what I wanted to say is…darling

Annie, I love you. Let me show you how much. Please come back to me. I can't live without you." He looked terrible, as if he hadn't slept in days. There were dark circles under his eyes and his face was haggard.

Despite everything, she couldn't help it, she felt sorry for him. "Look, Jonathan," she said as gently as she could manage, "I know you think—"

"I'm begging you," he cried, interrupting her. "I've changed. I have. I'll never hurt you again. I promise. I'll do anything you want if you'll only let me come back. I'll go to a counselor, whatever you want me to do. Just come back to me." His blue eyes pinned hers. "I can't stand it without you. I can't eat. I can't sleep. All I think about is you and how stupid I was and how much I love you."

She held up her hands. "Jonathan, stop. Please stop. I can't do this."

"Please, Annie. I've changed! Why are you being so hard? You never used to be so hard."

"I'm not being hard. I...I just—" she took a deep breath "—I don't love you anymore."

"You don't mean that. I know you don't. You're just saying it to punish me. Well, you're right. I deserve to be punished. Here." He stuck out his jaw. "Hit me. Go ahead. Punch me as hard as you can. Just don't say you don't love me."

"Stop it, Jonathan! Just stop it."

Pulling back, he stared at her.

"I don't want to hurt you," she said softly. "But

you've got to face the truth. I don't love you anymore, and I'm not coming back.''

''I told you not to say that!''

He grabbed her by the shoulders, and she winced. His grip was strong. She closed her eyes. *Please God,* she prayed. *Make him understand. Make him go away.*

''I'll get my vasectomy reversed.'' His voice rang in desperation. ''We'll have children. As many as you want. Just come home where you belong.''

''I can't,'' she whispered.

His hands tightened, and pain shot down her arms. ''You mean you won't.'' The begging tone had disappeared.

From somewhere, Annie summoned the strength to meet his gaze squarely. ''That's right. I won't. I'm sorry, but nothing you say is going to change my mind. Our marriage is over.''

His eyes slowly darkened in fury. ''You bitch,'' he said through gritted teeth.

When he abruptly released her shoulders, she thought he had finally accepted the truth and was going to leave. So she wasn't prepared for the blow to the chest. He punched her so hard she lost her balance and fell heavily, striking her head on the corner of the coffee table.

Just before she lost consciousness, she saw him draw back his foot to kick her.

A moment later the world turned black.

Chapter Two

The windshield wipers of Kevin Callahan's Ford pickup truck were turned on high, but it was still hard to see. This was one of the worst spring storms the hill country had experienced in years. The rain was actually blowing sideways, and according to the radio reports, some areas were getting hail.

He slowed down. He was in no hurry to get home. It wasn't as if he had anything special to look forward to.

Kevin hated the weekends. During the week he was busy, and so was everyone else. But the weekends…that was when couples did things together. That was when the loneliness seemed almost unbearable, and nothing his family ever planned to take his mind off his loss did anything to alleviate it more than temporarily.

Jill, I miss you so much.

The pain wasn't as bad as it had been, but Kevin knew it would never go away entirely. He didn't even want it to go away, because if it did, that would mean the memory of what they'd had together would have faded, too.

It was ironic. Until he was almost forty years old, he'd never believed he was the marrying kind. He'd looked at the marriages of his parents and his brothers and sister with a kind of awe. He'd figured he would never find anyone who could inspire that kind of commitment.

And then he'd met Jill and everything he'd ever believed about himself changed. They'd become engaged after only three months and set a wedding date for eight months after that. They'd been so happy. Kevin had never believed he could *be* so happy. And then, in one horrible moment, she had been taken away from him, killed in an automobile accident just six weeks before their wedding. Those weeks after her death were a blur. Kevin had been numb, totally stunned by pain and grief.

It had been a year now, and still he sometimes found it hard to believe she was actually gone. Today she'd been on his mind a lot, because he'd spent the morning in Austin finalizing plans for his new office. She would have been so proud, he thought wistfully, picturing the gold lettering on the door.

Kevin Callahan, Architect.

Hanging out his shingle would be the fulfillment of a long-held dream. And now there was no one with whom to plan and share the excitement.

Jill...

He was so lost in his thoughts he almost missed seeing the girl. But suddenly there she was, weaving and stumbling along the road. If his reflexes hadn't been as good as they were, he would have hit her. As it was, he had to swerve sharply, nearly losing control of the truck as it skidded sideways on the wet pavement.

"What the *hell?*" Heart pounding, he finally brought the truck to a stop. In his rearview mirror, he could see that the girl now lay in a heap on the ground. He swore. Had he hit her after all?

Grabbing the big black umbrella he kept in the truck, Kevin leaped out and raced toward her. What she was doing wandering in a torrential rainstorm on a nearly isolated two-lane road where there were no houses for miles, he couldn't imagine. Was she sick? Stoned? Crazy?

Reaching her side, he knelt next to her. "Miss?" he said gently, touching her shoulder. He put the umbrella over her to shield her from the rain. "Are you okay?"

Her eyes fluttered open. "I...I—" Her teeth chattered, and she struggled to sit up, but the effort obviously exhausted her, for she fell back, and her eyes closed again.

This time when Kevin spoke to her, there was no response at all. Alarmed, he knew he had to get her off the road and into the truck. But managing that while holding the umbrella was impossible. So he closed the umbrella and tossed it down, then lifted her up and into his arms. She hardly weighed anything, and he easily carried her over to the passenger side. He even managed to get the door open without too much difficulty, then he gently eased her inside. Once she was safely in, he ran back to retrieve the umbrella. By now he was as soaked as she was, but he hardly noticed. He was totally focused on getting the girl some help, because it was evident she was either hurt or ill.

The logical place to take her was the emergency room at Tri-City General, the hospital that served Rainbow's End, Pollero and Whitley, neighboring towns that had banded together to provide services none could have afforded or adequately supported on its own.

He debated calling 911 on his cell phone, but reasoned it would be faster to just drive her there rather than call an ambulance which would have twice as much distance to travel with a round trip.

Kevin drove carefully. The last thing he wanted was to have an accident. He *had* managed to get the seat belt around the girl, who was slumped against the door, so at least she was afforded some protection. He couldn't tell if she was unconscious or not.

She still didn't answer him when he questioned her, so he was assuming she was.

It didn't take long to reach the hospital. Kevin always felt a sense of pride when he saw the constantly growing facility, which had been built by Callahan Construction Company, the business his father had started and which had grown into one of the area's largest employers.

Pulling into the turnaround by the emergency room entrance, Kevin turned off the ignition, got out and raced around to the driver's side to get the girl. She roused briefly as he lifted her out, but her eyes closed again as he carried her inside.

The triage nurse looked up at his entrance. She seemed startled as her blue eyes met his.

Kevin recognized her as Jackie Fox, a girl he'd dated a half dozen years ago. "Hey, Jackie." Briefly he described how he'd found the girl in his arms.

Jackie immediately sprang into action. "Let's get her back into one of the treatment rooms," she said crisply. "We'll need to get her out of her wet clothes and see if we can figure out what's wrong with her."

Once the girl was lying on an examining table, Kevin got his first good look at her. She was older than he'd first thought, he realized as Jackie dried her face and, with Kevin's help, removed her raincoat. Not a teenager at all. In fact, maybe late twenties or early thirties. Her hair looked to be a dark blond or light brown, but it was hard to tell since it was so wet. He wasn't sure from the brief glimpse he'd had of them, but he thought her eyes were brown. She was a pretty girl, or would have been if she didn't look so pale and fragile.

When Jackie had finished taking the girl's blood pressure and pulse and listening to her heart, she pulled a blanket from the shelf and covered her. "Keep an eye on her. I'll get Dr. Sanchez."

While Jackie was gone, Kevin studied the girl's face. It was a delicate face with fine bones, a small, tip-tilted nose, wide mouth and nicely shaped ears set close to her head. As he stood there, she began to stir, and her eyelids fluttered open. Her eyes— he'd been right, they were brown with gold flecks— were unfocused at first, but gradually they homed in on Kevin.

"Hi." He smiled down at her.

She frowned. "H-hi."

He was glad to see she didn't seem afraid of him. When she tried to raise herself up, he touched her shoulder. "Don't try to sit up. Wait until the doctor gets here."

"D-doctor?"

"Yes. You're at Tri-City General." When that information elicited no sign of recognition, he added, "The hospital that serves Rainbow's End, Pollero and Whitley?"

Her frown deepened. She shook her head, then winced and put her hands to her forehead. "I d-don't understand.'' With each word she sounded more agitated.

''Maybe it's best if you don't try to talk.'' Kevin wished Jackie would get back quickly.

''B-but h-how did I get here…?''

''I brought you.''

''You brought me? B-but I don't know you.''

''I know. You were on the road—''

He never had a chance to finish, because just then Jackie, accompanied by a young, harried-looking doctor with disheveled black hair, walked in. Kevin sighed with relief.

''She's awake, I see,'' Jackie said. She nodded toward Kevin. ''He brought her in.''

''I'm Dr. Sanchez,'' the man said.

''Kevin Callahan.''

They shook hands briefly, then Sanchez turned to the girl. He listened to her heart, examined her eyes, then put his arm under her to raise her up. When he did, she winced and moaned.

''Where does it hurt?''

''Everywhere. M-my head and my ch-chest and my s-stomach,'' she whispered.

Sanchez gently examined her head. ''Yes,'' he said, looking at the back. ''You have a pretty nasty bump there. What happened? Did you fall?''

''I…I don't know.''

Sanchez's eyes met Jackie's for a brief moment. Then he turned his attention back to the girl. ''Let's look at your chest.'' He unbuttoned her blouse and probed. ''Can you take a deep breath?''

She grimaced. ''It hurts.''

''Did someone hit you?'' he said bluntly.

''I...I don't remember.''

He looked skeptical. ''You don't remember? Or you're protecting someone?''

''Doctor,'' Kevin interjected, ''I think she's telling you the truth.'' He went on to explain how he'd happened upon her, all the time giving her reassuring glances. When he'd finished, Sanchez turned back to the girl.

''What's your name, Miss?''

At this, the girl's expression, which had only been confused, now began to look panicked. She bit her bottom lip and looked from Jackie to the doctor to Kevin. Suddenly her eyes filled with tears. ''I don't know.'' Putting her hands over her face, she started to cry.

''It's okay,'' Jackie said, putting her hand on the girl's shoulder in a comforting gesture. She frowned at the doctor.

Sanchez looked at Kevin. ''So you don't know who she is, either?''

Kevin shook his head. ''I was just driving home. She was wandering in the road...in the rain.''

Sanchez shook his head. ''I'm going to order a CT scan. Check out that lump at the back of her head. She might have a cracked rib, as well.'' He turned to Jackie. ''In addition to the CT scan, let's do some bloodwork.'' He reached for the chart and scribbled as he continued to give Jackie instructions.

When he was finished and had gone, Jackie pulled Kevin off to the side, out of the girl's earshot. ''Did she have a purse on her? Any ID?''

Kevin shook his head. ''Not that I could see.''

''Can you stick around? We need to talk, but first I'd like to call for someone in radiology to come and get her.''

''Sure, I'll wait.'' Even if he'd had plans for the evening, something about this girl and her dilemma wouldn't have allowed him to abandon her until he knew she was going to be okay.

The girl had finally calmed down and was lying back on the examining table with her eyes closed. Kevin felt sorry for her. It must be damned scary not to remember your name or how you got where you were. Not to mention how she had happened to get hurt.

The radiology attendant arrived within ten minutes of Jackie's call. Between him and Jackie, they settled the girl into a wheelchair, and soon she was taken away.

''Okay,'' Jackie said. ''Let's look at that raincoat of hers. Maybe there'll be some ID in the pockets.''

But all the pockets elicited were a couple of crumpled dollar bills, a tube of lip balm and a wadded-up tissue.

''I guess there's no way to tell if she's got any insurance,'' Jackie said.

"Look, don't worry about that. I'll pay whatever it costs to take care of her." Four years ago, Kevin wouldn't have been able to be so magnanimous, but ever since his windfall in the stock market, he had more money than he'd ever dreamed of.

"You sure? We can admit her as a charity case."

"I'm sure." For some reason Kevin felt responsible for the girl, even though he knew he had no further obligation toward her.

"Okay. I'll go get the paperwork ready. I'll need you to sign some stuff."

"Fine."

While Jackie went off to take care of the paperwork, Kevin took out his cell phone. He'd halfheartedly told his brother Rory he might come to Pot O' Gold, a favorite hangout of his two single brothers, later that evening, but now he had the perfect excuse not to go.

"Hey, man," Rory said when he answered. "We still on for tonight?"

"No, I don't think so."

"Why not?"

Kevin explained what had happened. "I'm going to stick around here until I find out how she's doing, and then I'm just going to go home and crash."

"You mean mope."

"Look, if I don't want—"

"Hey, save it, okay? This is your brother you're talking to. I know exactly what you're gonna do. It's what you've been doing ever since Jill died. Listen, Kev, she wouldn't want you to do this. She'd be the first one to say you gotta move on, put it behind you, start livin' again.''

Kevin wanted to tell him to mind his own business, but he knew that would be unfair. His family cared about him. They were only looking out for his best interests. What they didn't understand was that he had to take each step when he was ready to take it, not when they thought he should.

''Look,'' he said, ''I gotta go. I'll talk to you tomorrow.''

Before Rory could object, Kevin cut the connection. Then he turned his cell phone off. If Rory or anyone else called, they could leave a message. That way he wouldn't have to justify anything or listen to any more well-meant but unwanted advice.

A few minutes later Jackie returned. For the next hour, Kevin signed the papers assuming financial responsibility for Jane Doe—which was the name Jackie had put down—then he killed the rest of the time by reading his new *Architectural Digest,* which had come yesterday and which he'd tossed into his briefcase.

Finally Jackie said Jane was on her way back from radiology. ''She'll be going to room 103 in the south wing. You can go over there if you want to see her.''

''What did the tests show?''

''The radiologist will meet you there and go over everything.''

So Kevin walked over to one south. Room 103 was a pleasant room painted in a soft shade of gray with a large window overlooking a tree-shaded courtyard. The rain had stopped, and watery afternoon sunshine striped the floor.

Kevin stood at the window and looked through the slatted blinds. Several hospital workers sat smoking on a stone bench in the middle of the courtyard. He grimaced. It always surprised him to see medical personnel smoking. Yet why should it? Human beings could know something was bad for them; that didn't mean they could control their appetites or overcome their weaknesses. Suddenly he grinned. He sounded like a philosopher. Wouldn't his brothers laugh?

I've changed. They don't realize that yet. They still think I'm the old Kevin, the one game for anything, the one who was never serious. But I'm no longer that man. Jill's the reason. Loving her made me grow up.

He was still thinking, still staring out the window when, a few minutes later, the same attendant who'd taken Jane to radiology wheeled her into the room. Her gaze immediately sought Kevin's, and he could see how frightened she still was.

Poor kid. He couldn't imagine what it felt like not to remember anything. He smiled reassuringly, suddenly glad he'd ordered a private room for her. Bad enough she had some form of amnesia, she sure didn't need some roommate asking her all kinds of questions she couldn't answer.

A short, redheaded nurse strode briskly into the room. She thanked the attendant, then her gaze moved to Kevin. "You the husband?"

"Uh, no, just a friend."

"Okay. How about stepping out into the hall for a while? I'll call you when she's settled."

Kevin gave Jane one more reassuring smile, then left her in the nurse's obviously capable hands. He'd only been waiting outside a few minutes when a tall, sandy-haired doctor approached. He nodded to Kevin, then started to enter the room.

"Doctor," Kevin said. "Are you the radiologist I was supposed to meet here?"

"Yes. I'm Dr. Mitchell. Are you related to the patient?"

"No." Kevin introduced himself, then gave the doctor a brief rundown on the girl inside and how he'd found her. "I feel responsible for her, though. Have you been able to determine what's wrong with her?"

"If you mean do we know why she can't remember anything, there *is* some bruising of the cerebral cortex, which will cause temporary amnesia."

"Temporary?" Kevin said, seizing on the most important word. "You're sure it's only temporary?"

"We can't be 100 percent positive about anything, but there's a good chance her memory loss *is* only temporary, yes."

"How long will this temporary amnesia last?"

"It's anybody's guess, but usually in cases like this, memory returns fairly quickly. Maybe not all at once. Sometimes the patient will have islands of memory—isolated incidents—before complete recall returns."

Kevin knew it was ridiculous to feel so relieved. After all, that girl inside was a stranger. Yet he *did* feel relieved. "What about her other injuries?"

"In addition to that nasty bruise on her head, she's got two cracked ribs. Nothing very serious, although the ribs will be painful for a few days."

The doctor excused himself and went inside, while Kevin continued to wait. Five minutes later he came back out saying, "It's okay for you to go back in."

When Kevin reentered the room, Jane wore a green hospital gown instead of the jeans and cotton shirt she'd come in with. She was in bed in a half-sitting, half-lying-down position.

"I've taped up her ribs and given her something for pain," the nurse said. Her no-nonsense gaze moved to Jane. "You're going to feel sleepy soon."

When the nurse was gone, Kevin pulled one of the two chairs in the room closer to the bed and sat down next to Jane, whose eyes still had a haunted look.

"I don't want you to worry," he said. "Everything's going to be okay."

She swallowed, but her eyes filled with tears again. "B-but I still can't remember anything."

"I know, but Dr. Mitchell said your memory loss is probably only temporary."

"He did?"

"Yes. He even said he thought it wouldn't take long for it to return."

She bit her bottom lip. "But what if he's wrong? What if my memory *doesn't* come back?" she whispered.

"Listen, worrying about this won't change anything. What you need to do now is put everything out of your mind and try to get some sleep. Things will look a lot better tomorrow. In fact, I wouldn't be surprised if you remember everything when you wake up."

Kevin would have said anything to wipe that frightened look off her face. Anyway, maybe he was right. Maybe she *would* remember everything tomorrow.

His words seemed to do the trick, because she nodded and leaned her head back. A few minutes later her eyes drifted shut, and soon she was breathing slowly and evenly. Kevin sat there for a while, until he was sure she wasn't going to wake up, then he rose, took one last look at her still form and quietly left the room.

Chapter Three

Kevin thought about the girl all the way home. He was sure glad he'd seen her. No telling what could have happened to her if he hadn't come along when he did. Even now he shuddered to think how close he'd come to hitting her.

What had caused her injuries? He knew the emergency room doctor suspected someone had beaten her, but maybe that wasn't the case at all. Maybe she'd fallen down the stairs or something. Still, it was puzzling that she was wearing a raincoat when he'd found her. He supposed it was possible she could have fallen outside, maybe knocked herself out, then when she came to, she was dazed and wandered off.

He was still thinking about her when he reached his house. As he pulled into the driveway, the sun was setting, and the western side of the house was gilded in orange and gold.

It was a terrific house, one that should have been a source of great pride—the physical proof that his dream of becoming an architect was now a reality and that he could and would design houses that were beautiful as well as functional. But Kevin's feelings about and pride in the house were bittersweet.

Jill had been so much a part of its design and development. Everything about it had been planned around the life they were going to share. Now that she was gone, much of the pleasure in the house was gone, too.

Still, it *was* beautiful—a multilevel marvel of ingenuity and charm. Although its ultramodern lines could have been stark and cold, it was saved by the warmth of the woods, colors and textures used throughout.

On the bottom level were the garage, storage room, laundry room, workshop and game room. The game room had been intended as a studio for Jill, who had been a talented sculptor, and even though it now contained a regulation-size pool table, Kevin could never forget its original purpose. Consequently he avoided it.

On the next level were the kitchen, dining room, living room, guest room and guest bath. The top level consisted of the master bedroom and bath and Kevin's office.

There were wraparound porches on levels two and three, and huge windows that overlooked the rolling hills that surrounded the house.

Kevin and Jill had intended to put in a pool, but that was another thing Kevin had lost all heart for.

Heaving a sigh, he pulled his truck into the garage and entered the house. He headed straight for the master bedroom. An hour later he had showered, changed into well-worn sweats and was in the kitchen. He poked through the refrigerator, finally deciding he'd just scramble some eggs and make some toast and call that his dinner.

Once it was ready, he carried his plate and a glass of cold milk into the living room. He put his food on the washed-pine coffee table, then sank down onto the six-foot-long navy leather couch.

He eyed the remote, but he wasn't in the mood to watch TV. That was the story of his life, he thought. Since Jill's death, he hadn't been in the mood for anything. For some reason this thought made his mind turn to Jane again. He thought about how he'd told her tomorrow would be a better day.

That was a joke. He had no idea if her tomorrows would be better. For all he knew, they could be worse. It wasn't like she, or anyone else, had any control over them. Hell, all of life was a crap shoot, and anyone who believed differently had a sad awakening coming sooner or later.

Kevin's mouth twisted, and the eggs he'd been mindlessly shoveling into his mouth suddenly tasted like straw. He put his fork down and pushed his plate away.

The last of the afternoon sun disappeared, and darkness crept into the room. Kevin sat for a long time. Maybe his tomorrows had been spoiled forever, but that didn't mean Jane's had to be, especially when he had the means to help her. He wasn't sure why he felt so strongly about this unknown woman, but he did, and he was going back to the hospital tomorrow.

Maybe it was nuts—he was sure his brothers would think so—but he couldn't help feeling there was a reason he'd been the one to find Jane.

Someone was chasing her. It was dark, and she was in some kind of alley, and she could hear feet pounding behind her, echoing the pounding of her heart.

She ran as fast as she could. Her heart was pumping hard, and her chest hurt, but she kept running, because she knew if she slowed down for even a minute, he would catch her. Yet no matter how fast she ran, she could hear her pursuer coming closer and closer.

Please, God, please, God, please, God.

She was so frightened. She had to get away. She had to! And then suddenly he was right behind her. His hands closed over her shoulders.

She screamed and jerked upright.

A second later light flooded the room. She looked around wildly. Where was she? She stared in terror at the woman in white who stood in the doorway.

"It's okay," the woman said. She was tall and black and had kind eyes. "You're in the hospital. You had a nightmare." She walked swiftly to the bedside. Her hands felt cool and gentle, comforting as they soothed.

The hospital? What was she doing in the hospital? She listened as the nurse explained what had happened the day before, and as the nurse talked, she remembered the man who'd brought her here. He'd said his name was Kevin. Kevin Callahan. It was a nice name. And he'd had a nice smile, too, as well as nice eyes. She remembered thinking that they were the bluest eyes she'd ever seen. He'd made her feel better even though she didn't know who she was or what she'd been doing wandering in the rain.

She clapped her hand over her mouth and began to tremble. *Oh, God...*

"Listen, hon," the nurse said, "I know you're scared, and I don't blame you, not at all. But whatever it is you were dreaming about can't hurt you now. Not here. You're safe here." She tucked the blanket more securely around her. "Tell me, are you hurting? Do you want something else for pain?"

"N-no. I—I'm all right." But she wasn't all right. How could she be? She had no idea who she was or what had happened to her. Her bottom lip trembled. *Who am I?* The hospital personnel were calling her Jane, because they had to call her something, but she knew that wasn't really her name. If only she could remember…

"Want me to leave the light on?"

"No," she whispered. She had to fight to keep from crying.

The nurse gave her another sympathetic smile, then left the room, switching off the light on her way out.

Jane closed her eyes and tried to calm herself so she could go back to sleep. But her mind wouldn't cooperate. The same questions kept going round and round in her brain.

Who am I? What happened to me?

Yet no matter how many times she asked herself the questions, there were never any answers. Finally, exhausted by the furious concentration and effort to remember that brought only a pounding headache and no answers, she slipped back into sleep.

Kevin had just finished drinking his second cup of coffee when the phone rang.

"I didn't wake you, did I?"

It was Jack Kinsella, his sister Sheila's husband and Kevin's best friend for most of his life.

"Nope. Been up since seven." He glanced at the wall clock. It was almost nine.

"Sheila said to invite you for dinner tonight. So I'm inviting you."

Kevin smiled. Ever since Jill's death, at least once a week, a dinner invitation came from the Kinsellas. "What's on the menu?"

"Your brother wants to know what's on the menu," Jack called out.

Kevin heard his sister talking in the background.

"She says we'll grill some steaks."

"I'll come, but on one condition."

"I know. You'll bring the steaks."

"That's right." Furnishing steak or shrimp or lamb chops was one of the few ways Kevin could repay them for their hospitality. At first they had given him an argument about bringing anything. Now they just let him contribute the food because they knew he wouldn't come otherwise.

"So what else have you got planned for today?" Jack asked.

"I'm going over to the hospital in a little while."

"Oh?"

Kevin explained what had happened the day before.

"So you don't know anything about this woman?" Jack asked when he'd finished.

"Nope."

"Hmmm."

"What?"

"Maybe it's not a good idea to get involved with her."

"I'm not getting involved. I'm just…"

"You're getting involved."

"I can't help it. I feel responsible." For one second he considered telling Jack that he also felt there was a reason he'd been the one to find Jane, but the urge passed.

"Maybe she's in trouble."

"You mean with the cops?" Kevin hadn't thought of that possibility. He frowned. Somehow Jane didn't seem like the type, but you never knew.

"Why don't you give Zach a call? He'd probably know."

"That's an idea," Kevin said thoughtfully. A few years ago, his cousin Maggie had married Zachary Tate, who was the county sheriff.

"Yeah, because if she's in some kind of trouble, you'd be better off not getting involved."

Jack was probably right, but Kevin didn't think he could just walk away. Hell, what could it hurt just to go see Jane this morning?

"So what about the office?" Jack said, obviously under the impression the subject of Jane had been settled. "Did you get everything done yesterday?"

"Mostly. The desks aren't in yet, but otherwise I'm in good shape." Kevin still had to hire a receptionist, but that could wait until he had some work lined up to justify the expense.

"That's good."

"All I need now is some work."

"That'll come. You've just got to give it some time."

"I know. I'm not worried."

"Well, I'd better let you get going. See you about six?"

"I'll be there."

They hung up, and Kevin hurriedly cleaned up his breakfast stuff, then was on his way. He arrived at the hospital thirty minutes later.

When he got to Jane's room he was surprised to find her dressed and sitting on a chair. She looked a lot better than she had the day before. Her hair— dark blond as he'd thought—was clean and brushed back, and she was even wearing some lipstick.

"Hi," he said.

Her quick smile said she was glad to see him. "Hi."

"Feeling better today?"

"Yes, a lot better." She grimaced. "I still don't remember anything, though. And…" The grimace turned to a worried frown. "They're saying I can go home today. But—"

Kevin immediately understood. "Don't worry." His mind raced. Where could she go? He'd willingly pay for a motel room, but that would be impersonal and lonely. And Jane needed to be with people who could help her. Suddenly he had it—a place his brother Patrick's wife, Jan, had mentioned many times.

"There's a great women's shelter here," he said. "My sister-in-law volunteers there. I know they'd be happy to have you stay with them until your memory comes back." He almost added, *or until someone comes looking for you* but thought better of it. No sense alarming her. She seemed smart enough to figure it out for herself.

"A *homeless* shelter?" She seemed upset.

"Some of the women are homeless, yes, but some come from abusive situations or have just had a run of back luck and need some temporary help."

She bit her bottom lip and looked down. After a few moments, she sighed. "I guess beggars can't be choosers."

Kevin almost said, *Oh, hell, you can stay in my guest room, if you want to,* but he stopped himself. That wasn't a good idea. He was right to steer her in this direction. She shouldn't be alone, and the personnel at the shelter were equipped to give her the emotional support she needed, and he sure as hell wasn't. "So what do we need to do about checking you out of here?"

"I'm supposed to ring for the nurse when I'm ready."

"What do you need to do to get ready?"

"Nothing. I was just waiting, hoping you'd come."

He could see it was hard for her to admit this, which made him doubly glad he'd decided to ignore Jack's admonition not to get involved. "Let's go, then."

He noticed she was moving gingerly as she collected her raincoat and a bag of hospital supplies that was sitting on the bed table. He was sure her chest still hurt. Cracked ribs were no small thing. "Did they give you a prescription for pain pills?"

She nodded.

"We'll fill it on the way."

"But I…"

"What?"

"I don't have any money," she said in a small voice.

"Look, it's no big deal. You'll pay me back when your memory returns."

"But I don't know when that's going to be, or even *if* I can pay you back. Maybe I don't have any money."

"I told you not to worry. The money's not important. What's important is getting you well."

"You don't even know me. Why are you being so nice?"

"Look, I've got a sister. If anything happened to her, I'd like to think someone would help her out."

She didn't reply for a moment. When she did, he saw that her eyes were shiny with tears. "Thank you," she whispered.

He patted her shoulder awkwardly.

Once she was checked out and Kevin had looked over the bill, they were on their way. "If anything jogs your memory and you want to stop, let me know," he said.

"All right."

But nothing did, and twenty minutes later, he pulled into the parking lot of the shelter.

Kevin had only been to the shelter once that he could remember, to deliver a box of toys that his father's employees had donated one Christmas, since many of the women at the shelter had small children. At the time he was favorably impressed by the place, which was colorfully decorated and cheerful.

Today, as they walked inside, he was glad to see nothing had changed. The reception area, although furnished with inexpensive-looking Scandinavian-influenced blond furniture, was painted a bright yellow, and the couch and chair cushions were a cheerful green-and-yellow plaid. The walls were covered with framed posters of famous landmarks like the Statue of Liberty and the Eiffel Tower and the Golden Gate Bridge.

A counter divided the room, with the reception area on one side and an office area on the other. A dark-haired, middle-aged woman with a pleasant face got up from her desk as they walked in.

"Hi," she said. "Can I help you?"

"Is Jan Callahan working today?" Kevin asked.

"No, sorry, Jan is only here on Thursdays."

"Okay, well…" He looked at Jane. "She needs a place to stay." Quickly he explained Jane's circumstances.

"Oh, hon," the woman said, giving Jane a sympathetic look, "that must be awful, not being able to remember anything."

"It's not great," Jane said.

"Why don't you two have a seat? I'll call the director and you can talk to her."

A few minutes later a door at the back of the office area opened and a tall, gray-haired woman walked in. She came out into the reception area. Kevin rose to his feet, and after a moment so did Jane.

"Hello," the woman said. "I'm Margaret Burke, the director of the shelter."

Kevin introduced himself and Jane and once more explained the circumstances that had brought them there.

"You're in luck today," the director said, "because we happen to have some space. One of our residents moved out this week and that's freed up a room."

Kevin hadn't realized there might be a chance they couldn't take her. What he would have done if the shelter hadn't had room he didn't know and was glad he hadn't been forced to find out.

"Bobbi here will give you the forms to fill out," the director continued. She gave Jane a sympathetic smile. "I realize you won't be able to give us much information, but do your best. When you're finished, Bobbi will bring you back to my office, and I'll show you around the center."

"May I come, too?" Kevin asked.

"Certainly."

After getting the paperwork filled out, Bobbi pressed something under the counter that sounded three bells. Then she unlocked the door that led to the inner section and beckoned them to follow.

"What did those three bells mean?" Kevin asked.

"It lets the women know a man is coming in," Bobbi explained.

That made sense, Kevin thought.

"We also have an alarm that would alert everyone to an unwanted visitor."

That made even more sense.

On the way to the director's office, Kevin saw a cafeteria, several lounge areas, a children's play area, a file room and several offices.

"Where are the bedrooms?" he asked.

"They are in another wing," Bobbi said. "Men aren't allowed back there." She stopped in front of a closed door and knocked.

"Come in."

Kevin and Jane were ushered into a large office cluttered with filing cabinets and a small desk, behind which Margaret Burke now sat. She waved them to two straight-backed chairs in front of the desk.

Once Bobbi had gone, Margaret said, "What do you think of our center?"

"It's very nice," Jane said politely.

"We're very proud of the work we do here. We've helped a lot of women get on their feet."

"H-how many women live here?" Jane asked.

"We have room for twenty-five."

"Does that include the children, too?" Kevin asked.

"No. We can also accommodate about twenty children. We're hoping to soon be able to handle more. If our fund-raising campaign goes well." Her gaze moved to Jane. "Is there anything else you'd like to know?"

Jane shook her head.

"Then I'll tell you about our rules, and when I'm done, I'll take you to see your room." She smiled at Kevin. "You'll have to wait here, I'm afraid. We don't allow men in the sleeping areas."

"Bobbi told me," he said.

"We don't ask a lot of our residents, but we do have strict rules about making beds, cleaning up after yourself and consideration of others. Everyone has kitchen duty and bathroom duty, according to a schedule that's given out each Sunday evening." Margaret continued to rattle off rules and regulations, but in a friendly way accompanied by a smile.

Even so, Kevin could see Jane was scared, and he didn't blame her. Soon he would be leaving, and even though she didn't know him well, at least he was a familiar face. But once he was gone, she would be surrounded by strangers. Yet what else could he do?

"We also have a supply of clothing and toiletries available. You can pick out whatever you need. We don't put any limitations on our residents in that regard."

"She doesn't need to do that," Kevin said. "I'll take her out to buy whatever she needs."

"No," Jane said quickly. "You've done enough." She looked at Margaret. "Thank you. I'll be happy to use whatever you'll let me have."

Kevin wanted to argue with her, but he could see by the look on her face that he would lose.

"If you're ready, I'll take you back and show you your room. And then, after Mr. Callahan leaves, I'll take you to the supply room."

"Can she have phone calls?" Kevin asked.

"Yes, of course, but unless it's really important, please don't call before eight or after nine at night."

"What about going out?" he asked.

"She's free to go wherever she pleases, as long as she's not on the duty roster."

"In that case…" He smiled at Jane. "How about if I go now, but come back about five-thirty? I'll take you out for dinner."

"You don't have to do that," Jane said. "I don't want you to feel responsible for me."

"I know I don't have to. I want to. This'll give us a chance to get to know each other better."

"Well…"

"I'll be here at five-thirty."

He had decided not to tell her they were going to Sheila and Jack's because he figured she might refuse to go. Once she was there, it would be too late to object.

"All right. Thank you."

Her smile made him feel good, and he was glad he'd had the idea to take her along tonight. He knew Sheila wouldn't mind. And what Jack thought was irrelevant. Kevin was an adult. He could make his own decisions. And if they turned out to be bad decisions, that was his problem and no one else's.

Sheila Callahan Kinsella looked around as the back door opened and her husband of five years walked in. "I thought you were going to work until three."

He shrugged. "It rained on us, so I sent the crew home."

"Really? It didn't rain here." She lifted her face for his kiss. No matter how long they were married, she knew she'd always feel this same thrill when she saw him after not seeing him for a while, even when it was only a matter of hours.

That she should feel this way was no surprise to her. She'd been in love with Jack since she was in high school. It had taken him a bit longer to wake up to the fact they belonged together, but then, most men were clueless.

"What kind of pie?" he said, looking at the pie crust dough she was in the process of rolling out.

"Banana cream."

He grinned. "My favorite."

"I know."

"Kids napping?"

"Rose is. Ryan's over at Keith and Susan's."

Jack slid his arms around her waist. He made a mock lecherous leer. "Ryan's away and Rose is asleep?" His voice was suggestive.

"Yesssss," Sheila said, chuckling as his hands moved up to cup her breasts. For a few seconds she closed her eyes and savored the sensation of happiness that enveloped her at her husband's caress. "But he'll be home soon."

Jack nuzzled her neck. "Tell me we have time for a quickie."

"Sorry, my love." She could feel his arousal against her. "Save that for later," she murmured.

"Killjoy." After another quick kiss, he released her. "Since my wife won't accommodate me, I guess I'll go with my second best option."

"A shower?"

Jack raised his arm. "Yup."

"Before you go, guess what?"

"What?"

"Kevin called earlier and wanted to know if it was all right to bring someone along with him tonight."

"You mean a *girl?*" Jack looked amazed. "Who?"

"He said he told you about her this morning. The woman he found on the road, the one he went to see at the hospital."

"I'll be damned."

"Yeah, that was my reaction."

"You think he's just being a Good Samaritan or do you think he's interested in her?"

"I don't know. He indicated she was scared and he felt sorry for her. I guess we'll have to wait and see what she's like and how he acts around her."

"I told him I didn't think it was a good idea to get involved with her," Jack said thoughtfully.

"You *did?*" Sheila was amazed. Her husband wasn't the kind to hand out advice unless he was asked. Even then he subscribed to the philosophy that most people didn't really want advice. They wanted you to tell them they were right about what *they* wanted to do. Which meant it was best to keep your mouth shut.

"Yeah, I should have known better," Jack said. "Tonight ought to be interesting."

After Jack left her, Sheila finished rolling out her dough and making her pie crust. She'd preheated the oven earlier, so while the pie crust baked, she began to assemble the ingredients for the cream filling.

While she worked, she thought about her brother and how, after Jill died, he'd been so despondent. They'd all been worried about him. Lately, though, he seemed much better, as if he was finally getting over losing Jill.

Sheila couldn't imagine what it must be like to lose the person you loved. She couldn't even bear to think about losing Jack. She smiled, thinking about later tonight, after Kevin and this girl he was bringing went home and the kids were asleep and she and Jack were finally alone in their big bed.

She sighed. She was so lucky. Before she and Jack were married, she had believed she was as happy as the next person. But now she knew what true happiness was. Having someone to love and be loved by, having two wonderful children and another on the way, that was true happiness.

She looked down at her still-flat stomach. Jack didn't know she was pregnant again. She'd only found out herself yesterday. She would tell him tonight when they were alone. She knew he would be glad. For the past couple of years they had not practiced any form of birth control, hoping for just this outcome. But unlike the other two, this baby had taken a while to conceive.

In fact, Sheila had begun to think it might not happen. But it had, and now Ryan, who was three and a half, and Rose, who had recently turned two, would have a new brother or sister.

She smiled contentedly. Three children. A perfect-size family.

Just then the oven dinged. Her pie crust was done, reminding her that she'd better stop daydreaming and finish her preparations for tonight.

Chapter Four

Jane sat on the bed and gazed around the spartan room. A single bed, a small dresser and matching chest, a nightstand, a wooden chair. That was it. Plain and functional with no frills.

When Margaret had brought her here earlier, they'd passed a dozen or so other bedrooms on the way. A few of the doors were open, so Jane had been able to see that most of the residents here had brought lots of personal items with them: gaily colored bedspreads and quilts, pretty lamps, rugs, toys, even some furniture, like rocking chairs or desks.

Somehow the fact that she had nothing with which to make this room personal brought home to her just how horrible her situation was.

She felt as if she were in the middle of a nightmare. It had to be a nightmare, because it couldn't be real. And yet she knew all of this *was* real, because she was real. If she wasn't, she wouldn't feel the pain in her chest or at the back of her head or in her stomach.

She didn't hurt as badly as she'd hurt yesterday, but it was still hard for her to take a deep breath.

She hugged herself. What had happened to her?

Why couldn't she remember?

The tears that had been sitting just below the surface, waiting to erupt at the slightest provocation, blurred her vision.

She swallowed. This brooding and feeling sorry for herself wasn't helping anything. She had to try to keep in mind what the radiologist had told Kevin. That when she least expected it, the memories would probably come back.

Of course, he hadn't been able to guarantee that's what would happen, but he'd been encouraging.

She sighed deeply and reminded herself that things *could* be a lot worse. At least she had a place to stay among people who seemed nice.

Count your blessings.

The thought startled her, because it had come from nowhere, as if someone had said it to her many times. For just a moment a memory flickered—a hazy memory of a smiling woman—but as quickly as it had come, it vanished.

Jane's hands trembled. Somehow she knew that

brief flash had given her a glimpse of someone she loved. Her mother? She squeezed her eyes shut and tried to bring the image back, but it wouldn't come, and eventually her shoulders sagged in defeat.

Yet the homey words remained.

Count your blessings.

Jane nodded, although there was no one to see her. Things could be worse. They really could. All she had to do was look around. Everyone she'd met here at the center had problems, some of them appearing to be much more serious than hers.

I'm alive. My injuries aren't life threatening. They're not even that serious. I have a safe, clean place to stay, food to eat, and I even have a friend. That thought made her smile. Kevin Callahan *was* a friend. Instinctively she knew it.

Feeling better now, she stood and tried to decide what to do with the afternoon, because she still had several hours before Kevin would return to pick her up for dinner. She'd already put away the clothing that she'd been given. Margaret had told her to rest, that tomorrow was soon enough to begin thinking about the future, but Jane wasn't tired.

Just then there was a knock at the door. She jumped. "Yes?"

The door opened, revealing a thin woman with wispy dark hair and a sweet smile. "Hi."

It was impossible not to smile back. "Hi."

"I'm Wanda."

"I wish I could tell you who *I* am, but I—I've lost my memory."

"I know," Wanda said kindly, "Margaret told us."

"They're calling me Jane. For Jane Doe."

Wanda nodded. "I thought you might be feeling scared. I know I was on my first day."

Jane didn't trust herself to speak. Those stupid tears were threatening again, and she didn't want to make a fool of herself in front of this woman.

"Anyway, I thought maybe you'd like to join us in the rec room. We're just sitting around talking and having soft drinks or tea."

Jane knew Wanda had seen the tears and was pretending she hadn't. "I don't know that I'd be very good company."

"Oh, come on. It'll be good for you to meet everyone. And believe me, they all understand exactly how you feel. We've all been there."

Jane knew she should go. Otherwise she would just sit there and worry for the entire three hours before Kevin arrived. She forced herself to smile again. "All right. I'll come."

In the rec room, which was the main gathering area at the center, there were about a dozen women. They stopped talking and looked around as she and Wanda entered. When Jane would have fallen back, Wanda wouldn't let her.

"Now c'mon," she said, "they won't bite."

All the faces *were* friendly, Jane saw. And behind the encouraging smiles, she also saw understanding. Yes, she thought in relief, everyone here knew about fear. The fears might be of different things, but that didn't matter. Fear was fear.

Immediately she felt so much better. Kevin and the doctor were right. Eventually she would remember who she was and where she'd come from. In the meantime here were women holding out a hand in friendship.

"Welcome," said a pretty young woman with curly dark hair who looked to be in her twenties. "I'm Ginny." She held out her hand, and Jane took it.

An older woman with gray hair and dark eyes half stood. She held out her hand, too. "I'm Barbara." Her voice was rough, as if she were a smoker.

The others chimed in one by one, introducing themselves with first names only. Lisa. Brigitte. Allison. Liz. Erin. Chris. Shari. Dawn. Kelly. Beth. Later Jane would find out that most of the women preferred not to use their last names. Because so many of them had been victims of abuse, they felt safer in anonymity.

When they'd finished introducing themselves, Jane's head was swimming.

Dawn, a tall redhead with an open, freckled face, laughed. "Don't try to remember all our names now. You'll gradually figure out who's who."

"Or she won't," said a quiet blonde who was visibly pregnant. Jane had already forgotten her name.

"This is a great place," said the girl who'd introduced herself as Brigitte. "I'm going to hate to leave." She was strikingly pretty, with long dark hair and beautiful big blue eyes.

"Where are you going?" Jane asked.

"Moving into my own apartment." She smiled proudly. "The people here helped me find a job, and I've saved up some money now, so it's time." She made a face. "It's kind of scary, though, going out on my own."

"You'll do fine," several of the women said in various ways.

"Everyone's scared when they first leave," Dawn said.

"But you have to move on," Wanda offered quietly. "I'm looking forward to being on my own again."

"Yeah, but you don't have to worry about child care," a tired-looking woman with brown hair said.

"True."

"Where *are* all the children?" Jane asked.

"On Saturday afternoons the volunteers entertain the kids," one of the women said.

Dawn explained. "Some of them have art classes, some have swimming, some go to movies, and the little ones play games and see videos."

"That's nice."

"Yes," Dawn agreed, "it is. Gives us a break."

"Margaret tells us you've lost your memory," Brigitte said.

Jane grimaced. "Yes."

"That's gotta *really* be scary," Dawn said. "Not knowing who you are or anything."

"Her memory will come back," Wanda said.

"Yeah," someone else chimed in, "remember that girl, her name was Karen. No. Karla. Yeah, that's it. Karla. She had amnesia, too. And she was only here, what? About a month? And her memory came back."

"Oh, yeah," said Dawn. "I remember her. That was last year, wasn't it?"

"Last *year?*" Jane said. Some of these women had been here more than a *year?*

Dawn saw her expression and made a face. "Allison and I have been back a couple of times. That's why we remember Karla."

Allison rolled her eyes. "Yeah, some of us never learn."

"What do you mean?" Jane asked.

"They mean that too many of us are here because we had violent domestic situations," Wanda said.

"Yeah, and some of us actually went back to the pigs," Allison said.

"*Went*," Dawn said. "Past tense."

"I hope you mean that," Brigitte said.

"I do."

"What about you, Jane?" the quiet blonde asked. "You married?"

Jane looked at her ringless left hand. "I don't think so."

"How would she *know,* Lisa?" Dawn said. "She lost her *memory,* remember?"

Everyone chuckled, and soon the subject turned to Lisa's pregnancy, and Jane was glad to no longer be the center of attention. She relaxed and listened, and before she knew it, two hours had gone by, and the group began to disperse.

As she prepared to return to her room and get ready for Kevin's arrival, she thanked Wanda for encouraging her to join them. "I really enjoyed meeting everyone and hearing what they had to say."

"Good. Feel better?"

"I do."

"Thing is," Wanda said, "everyone here is supportive of everyone else, 'cause we've all got problems."

Back in her room Jane looked through the clothing she'd chosen from the supply available to the residents. She'd been able to find a pair of jeans that fit reasonably well and a pair of khaki pants, in addition to several T-shirts and sweaters. She'd also found a really nice black skirt and some black flat shoes that were in fairly decent condition.

For the evening she decided on the jeans—her own needed laundering—and a short-sleeved emerald-green sweater that looked almost new. After changing, she brushed her hair, put on a bit more lipstick, then reached for her raincoat and headed out to the reception area. It was only five-twenty, but just in case Kevin came early, she wanted to be ready.

She didn't have to wait long. She'd only been sitting a couple of minutes when the outer door opened and Kevin walked in.

He smiled when he saw her sitting there. "Good. You're ready."

"Yes."

He looked at Candy, the volunteer currently manning the reception desk. "What time do I have to have her back?"

"This door is locked at eight," Candy said, "but if you buzz, someone will be available to let you in up until midnight. After midnight, the place is a fortress and only emergency personnel are admitted."

After hearing some of the women's stories today, Jane understood why they were cautious. The door leading from the reception area to the inner sanctum of the shelter was always kept locked, too. You could get out, but no one could get in unless they had a key.

"Okay," Kevin said. "Ready to roll?"

It surprised Jane to feel how warm it was when they walked outside. The cool weather from yesterday's rain had totally disappeared and now it really felt like spring, with a soft breeze under clear skies. Her raincoat was unnecessary. She took a deep breath, forgetting it hurt to do so, and was immediately sorry.

"What's wrong?" Kevin asked.

"I just forgot it hurt to take a deep breath."

He gave her shoulder a sympathetic squeeze, but didn't say anything more, and Jane was glad. She didn't want to talk about her injuries. She didn't want to talk about anything that reminded her of her situation. For tonight she just wanted to pretend she was a normal person, going out for a normal evening with a friend.

"I'm not taking you to a restaurant," Kevin said once they were in his truck and on their way.

With anyone else, Jane might have felt a flicker of unease, but even though she didn't know much about this man, she had no doubt she could trust him. After all, he'd practically saved her life yesterday, hadn't he? From what she'd been told, she could have been hit by a car, that's how dazed and erratic she'd been. Instead this man had stopped and been caring enough to take her to the hospital and see that she was treated. Not only that, he'd *paid* for the treatment.

That fact bothered Jane. Somehow she knew she wasn't the sort of person who expected a handout, and she'd already promised herself that just as soon as she recovered her memory, she would pay every penny back.

So his announcement about not taking her to a

restaurant didn't alarm her, and all she said was, "Oh? Where *are* we going?"

"To my sister's house." He gave her a quick, sidelong look. "You'll like her. Her husband's been my best friend since we were little. And they have two of the cutest kids you'll ever meet."

Even though Jane did feel some qualms about having to face more questions and curious looks, she would never have said so, not to him. She owed him too much. "I'm looking forward to meeting them."

They fell silent after that, but it was a companionable silence, and she enjoyed looking out the window and seeing what the town looked like. It was a nice town, she thought. Clean and well kept with lots of trees and flowers. They passed what she imagined was the town square, because there was a courthouse there as well as different kinds of businesses. In the middle of the square was a statue of a man, and planted all around the statue were hundreds of bluebonnets in full bloom.

"Do you recognize anything?" Kevin asked.

The question startled her. "No."

"Too bad. I was hoping something might jog your memory."

She shook her head. "I...I don't think I've ever been here before. Of course, I can't be certain. It is a lovely town, though."

He smiled. "Yeah, everyone who visits seems to think so."

"Don't you?"

The smile became a grin. "When you live some-where, you hardly ever think about it. I mean, it's your home."

"I'm curious about the name Rainbow's End. Where does it come from?"

"My great-great grandfather named the town."

"Really?"

"Yep."

"How did that come about?"

"Well, he was looking for a place to settle and he rode over the hill leading into our valley. It had been raining, but it had stopped, and just as he hit the crest of the hill, a rainbow appeared. Both the rain and the rainbow reminded him of Ireland—you know it rains a lot in Ireland, right?"

Jane nodded. "Yes. I'd heard that." Funny, she might not know her name or anything about herself, but she did know about Ireland.

"Anyway, he knew he'd found the place he wanted to settle. So he staked his claim, built his house, and called the area Rainbow's End."

Jane smiled. She liked the story. "So your family was the first family here?"

"Yep. Callahans settled the town. My great-great-grandfather and his mother, Deirdre. In fact, that statue in the town square? That's him. Padriac Cal-lahan."

"And he brought his mother with him? What about his father?"

"His family emigrated from Ireland and originally settled in New York. But they didn't have good luck there. His father died in an accident on the wharves, so he and his mother decided to come west. They wanted a better life and more opportunities.''

''And they found them here.''

''Yes. Texas was good to them. We Callahans have prospered here.''

Jane wondered if she would ever know these kinds of things about her own family. She wanted to ask him more about his ancestors, but just then he pulled into the driveway of a two-story Colonial home in a pleasant subdivision.

The home was very welcoming, even from outside. You could tell children lived there. A tricycle lay upended on one side of the drive, and when Kevin opened the back gate, saying, ''Family doesn't use the front door,'' a swing set and sandbox were visible in the backyard.

The gate barely closed behind them when the back door opened. The young woman who stood framed in the doorway looked so much like Kevin, Jane would have guessed they were related even if she hadn't been told this was his sister's home. She wasn't as tall as her brother, but she had the same shining, almost black hair, and although her eyes were gray instead of the vivid blue of Kevin's, they were just as big and just as bright. Jane wondered what their parents looked like. They must be good-looking, because Kevin and his sister certainly were.

Her smile was just as warm as his, too.

"Hello," she said, turning that smile in Jane's direction. "I'm Sheila Kinsella. Welcome to our home."

Kevin hugged his sister, saying, "Hey, squirt, how's it going?"

Sheila grimaced. "Now, I ask you, how do you think it's going with two kids under the age of five?"

But the grimace quickly became a chuckle, and Jane knew that Sheila loved being a mom. She also saw, just from the way Kevin and Sheila talked to each other, that they were close. She couldn't help the envy that stabbed her. Right now she felt so alone. She wondered if she had any brothers and sisters, and if she did, if they had this kind of easy, warm relationship.

Surely, though, if she *did* have siblings, someone would be looking for her. Wouldn't they? The thought brought a comforting feeling of hope. Someone *must* be looking for her.

By now they had moved inside the house. A quick look around showed Jane a good-size, cheerful kitchen done in blues and yellows. A dimpled girl with curly, dark hair and bright-blue eyes who looked to be about two sat at the maple table. She was messily eating a cut-up peach.

"Unca Kevin!" she shouted, her mouth full of fruit.

"Rose," Sheila chided, "don't talk with your mouth full."

Kevin walked over and kissed his niece on the top of her head. "How's my Rosie-Posy?"

Rose grinned. "Wanna piece?" She held up a dripping wedge of peach.

Kevin returned the grin. "No, thanks, sweet thing. I'll pass."

"Rose, say hello to Jane," Sheila said.

"Hi, Rose," Jane said.

The girl ducked her head shyly. "Hi."

She was adorable, Jane decided as she watched Rose keep peeking out from under her eyelashes, even as she continued to stuff the last two pieces of dripping peach into her mouth.

"Where's Jack?" Kevin asked.

"He'll be down in a minute. He offered to bathe Ryan, so I took him up on it." Turning to Jane, Sheila explained, "Ryan's our son. He's three and a half. Rose is two."

"Two," Rose repeated. She held up two sticky-looking fingers. "Look, Mommy. Two."

"Yes, sweetie, I know. Two."

"Two *fingers*."

Sheila gave Jane an amused look. "You're right. That's two fingers."

Just then the timer on the oven dinged, and Sheila said, "Kev, why don't you take Jane into the living room and fix her something to drink. You know where everything is. I'll be in after I take my potatoes out of the oven and clean up my messy daughter.''

"I not messy," Rose said.

"That's a matter of opinion," Sheila said.

Jane followed Kevin down a short hallway into the large living room. It, too, looked cheerful and lived-in. At one end was a large brick fireplace, and the furniture was practical and comfortable looking. Family pictures adorned the walls and mantel, a sewing basket sat next to a wine-colored wing chair, the coffee table was home to a couple of children's books and, to Jane's delight, a sleek black cat sat on the windowsill of the big bay window that faced the front of the house. "Oh, I love cats," she said.

Kevin gave her a curious look. "Do you?"

She nodded slowly. "Yes. I don't know how I know that, but I do."

He smiled. "I have a feeling your memory's going to come back soon."

"I hope so." She walked over to the cat, who allowed Jane to pet its head. "You sure are a pretty one."

"That's Rabbit," Kevin said. "He rules the roost here."

Jane laughed. "Rabbit?"

"I know, ridiculous name for a cat, isn't it?"

"It *is* strange."

"The reason we call him Rabbit," said Sheila who, with Rose in tow, had just walked into the room, "is because my husband read this book to our son when he was two years old. It was about a rabbit, and afterward, Ryan kept asking for a rabbit. So one day Jack brought the cat home and told Ryan here was his rabbit.'' Sheila grinned. ''Jack said there was no way he was having a real rabbit in the house. They eat house plants and get into all kinds of mischief.''

''Pretty clever,'' Jane said. Rabbit arched his back and purred as she continued to pet him and scratch behind his ears.

''Kevin,'' Sheila said, ''you haven't given her anything to drink. What would you like, Jane? A soft drink, a glass of wine, a beer? I can even offer you a Bloody Mary or a rum and cola.''

''Maybe a glass of wine,'' Jane said. She had a feeling she wasn't much of a drinker.

''Red or white?''

''Red, I think.''

''I'll get it,'' Kevin said. ''What about you, Sheila?''

''I'll have a glass of wine, too.''

While Kevin fixed their drinks, Jane looked at the family portraits, and Sheila identified everyone. Wow, Jane thought as she studied one of Sheila and her husband and children. Jack Kinsella was every bit as good-looking as Kevin. And Ryan was just as adorable as his baby sister, although his hair was light brown.

''He takes after his grandmother Kinsella,'' Sheila said.

Jane was particularly fascinated with the large portrait that sat over the fireplace mantel.

"That's the entire Callahan clan," Sheila said.

"There are so many of you," Jane said. Once more, she felt that stab of envy. She hoped when she did regain her memory she would find she came from a large family, too. "Who are all of them?"

Sheila laughed. "Sure you want to know?" She pointed to each person. "Those are my parents, and there are Jack and the kids and me. They look younger, of course, because the portrait was taken two years ago at Christmas. And that's my oldest brother, Patrick, and his wife, Jan, and their four daughters. Aren't they beautiful? I can hardly believe Jana is twenty." Sheila smiled. "She's the oldest. I remember the day she was born. I thought my mother would die of excitement. Her first grandchild, you know." Sheila's smile turned soft. "She still gets just as excited over every new baby, though. I don't think she'll ever get bored with another grandchild."

"She's lovely," Jane murmured.

"My mother? Or Jana?"

"Both of them."

"Jana and Katie..." Sheila pointed to the girl standing next to Jana, "are both at UT in Austin. Jana's a junior, Katie's a freshman."

Jane nodded.

Sheila turned back to the portrait and pointed to another tall, dark-haired, handsome man. "And that's Keith, he comes third in the pecking order of my brothers. That's his wife, Susan, and their two children. Then there's Rory, he's not married, and Glenn, he isn't, either.'' She laughed. ''But we're working on *that!* Standing next to Glenn is Kevin. And that's my aunt Maureen—she was married to my dad's brother, Sean, who died about five years ago—and her son, Jimmy, and his wife, Molly, and their three children. And the tall redhead is her daughter, Maggie, and that's Maggie's husband, Zach. Zach is the sheriff here. And those are his three children from his first marriage.''

Jane just kept staring at the picture. So many people. And they all seemed so close and loving and happy. She wondered what it would be like to be part of a family like this one. To know that there were so many people in the world who cared about you.

''Kind of overwhelming, isn't it?'' Kevin said, walking up behind her.

Jane turned. ''Actually, I'm envious.''

He looked at her for a moment. ''Hey, you're going to remember your family,'' he said softly.

''I hope so.'' There was a hollow feeling in the pit of her stomach, and suddenly she wished she hadn't come with him tonight. She didn't belong here. Kevin wasn't her friend; he was just a kind stranger who had taken pity on her, and thinking anything else wasn't realistic. Nor was becoming dependent on him for anything. She wondered if she could possibly pretend to be sick so she could leave, because the idea of making small talk with him and his sister and her husband was no longer appealing. She wasn't even sure she *could* do it.

"What?" he said. "Is something wrong?"

She swallowed. "I...I feel kind of sick to my stomach."

He frowned, and Sheila's smile faded into a look of such concern that Jane was ashamed of herself.

"Oh, Jane," she said, "I'm so sorry. Would you like to lie down? Or can I get you something? A painkiller, maybe?"

"No, I..." Jane stopped. "It's okay. I just felt funny for a minute. I'll be okay."

"Are you sure?"

"Yes. I'm sure."

"Well, at least sit down." Sheila gestured to the sofa, which was deep cushioned.

As Jane settled herself and took a sip of her wine, she knew there was no way she could leave before Kevin was ready to go. She would eat the dinner so generously offered, she would talk and smile and accept the hospitality of Kevin's family, and if it had been offered because they felt sorry for her, so what? These were good people, and the least she could do as a thank-you to Kevin for everything he'd already done for her, was to be a gracious and appreciative guest.

But she also knew that being here with them was not her reality. No matter how appealing Kevin was and no matter how tempting it might be to lean on him, she couldn't.

Whatever her problems were, after tonight, it was not up to him to solve them, it was up to her.

Chapter Five

Kevin was glad he and Jack didn't have a chance
for a private word together. He wasn't in the mood
for a lecture. Oh, hell, that probably wasn't fair. Jack
never lectured. But Kevin knew he was wondering
what had changed since their conversation earlier
today and why Kevin had invited Jane to come with
him tonight, because Jack kept giving him speculative looks.

About midway through dinner, Kevin realized he
had made a mistake in bringing her tonight. Not for
the reason Jack had given him, but because it was
stupid to expect Jane to enjoy an evening with people she didn't know, no matter how nice they were.

She was trying. Kevin would give her that. She

was trying hard. But he could see she was having a tough time, and no wonder.

Damn. What *had* he been thinking, bringing her here? How could he imagine she would be able to relax and have fun? She had no idea who she was or where she'd come from or why she'd been injured. She was torn up inside, just as much as she was on the outside. Hell, if he were in her position, he wasn't sure he could even *pretend* to be having a good time.

He could have kicked himself for being so insensitive. He should have just taken Jane somewhere quiet for dinner. If he'd been using his head, he would have.

So as soon as they'd had their dessert—banana cream pie, Sheila's specialty—he followed his sister into the kitchen on the pretext of helping her carry the plates.

When they were out of hearing distance of Jack and Jane, he said, "Listen, Sheila, I know you suggested a game of Scattegories, but I think I should take Jane back to the center."

Sheila nodded. "Yeah, you're right. She's making a real effort, but I can tell she's uncomfortable...and probably exhausted from trying to pretend otherwise."

Kevin gave her a shoulder hug and kissed her temple. "Thanks, squirt."

Sheila swatted him with a dish towel. "You know I hate that name." But she was laughing.

Kevin waited until he'd been back in the living room awhile before suggesting they leave. He made his voice casual. "You know, I'm really beat. Jane, would you mind if we skipped the game and headed on back?"

"No, of course not."

"What about you, Sheila?"

"Don't be silly."

"Jack?"

"You kidding?" Jack said. "It's already past *my* bedtime."

Kevin rolled his eyes. "Boy, have things changed since you got married. I can remember when you were just getting started at midnight."

Jack smiled. "That was in the days when there was nothing at home in my lonely bed but me." He put his arm around Sheila.

The look Sheila gave Jack caused Kevin to feel a stab of pain, because it reminded him of Jill and the way she used to look at him. He wondered if he would ever be able to see happy couples without thinking of her.

He forced the thought away and looked at Jane. "You sure you don't mind going back this early?"

"No, not at all. The truth is, I'm tired myself."

He could see the relief in her eyes, and knew he'd done the right thing.

"I did have a lovely time, though," she said to Sheila. "I can't thank you enough for having me."

"It was our pleasure."

They said their goodbyes, and ten minutes later, they were on their way back to the center. Kevin wondered if he should say something to Jane, maybe apologize. While he was still trying to decide, she beat him to it.

"I'm sorry about tonight, Kevin. I know I wasn't very good company."

"You have nothing to apologize for. I shouldn't have dragged you there."

"You didn't drag me there."

"I sure didn't give you a choice. I wasn't thinking of how tough it would be for you to spend an evening with strangers."

"Please, Kevin, I mean it. I don't want you to feel bad. You were just being nice, trying to make me forget about my situation. I know that. And I appreciate it. I just…well, it was hard sitting there. I…the trouble is, I don't belong anywh-where."

Her voice wobbled, and he knew she was struggling to keep her composure. Pity flooded him.

"I don't know what I'm going to do," she said in a voice thick with tears. "What if I *don't* remember? I'm so scared."

"Aw, Jane…" They were on a residential street, so Kevin pulled to the curb and turned off the ignition. He turned sideways, leaning against the door so he could face her. "I don't blame you for being scared. You'd be stupid not to be. But it's too soon to worry. The doctor told you it might be a while, and I think he was telling you the truth when he said he felt your memory would come back.''

She bowed her head. ''But what if it doesn't?'' she whispered.

''We'll deal with that when the time comes.'' The *we'll* just seemed to come out of his mouth naturally.

''But I...I can't live at the shelter forever.''

''You won't have to. I'll help you find a place of your own.''

Her head turned slowly. In the dim light of the cab, her eyes glistened. ''I can't impose on you anymore, Kevin. You've already done too much.''

''Let me be the judge of that.''

''But—''

''Look. Give it a few days. If nothing happens during that time, if no one comes looking for you, and if you still can't remember anything, then we'll talk again. In the meantime, quit worrying. Okay?'' When she didn't answer, he said, ''Okay?'' more insistently.

She sighed deeply. ''Okay.''

He squeezed her shoulder. ''Trust me. Everything is going to be all right.''

Then he turned the key in the ignition and drove slowly back to the center.

Each day when Jane awakened, it took a few minutes before she realized where she was and why. Once she did, she found it hard to remain upbeat.

By the end of the week she knew she had to do something. She couldn't spend the rest of her life waiting for something to happen. She had to make it happen. Her injuries were healing nicely. It was time for her to get a job.

Later that morning, when Kevin called to check on her, she told him she was going to talk to Margaret and why.

"Before you do, let me check on something," he said.

"What?"

"I may know of a job."

"What kind of job?"

"Let me make a call first. It may not work out, so there's no sense talking about it now. If it does, I'll tell you all about it."

"All right. I can't talk to Margaret until Monday, anyway. She's out of town and won't be back until Sunday night."

After they'd hung up, Jane wondered if she should have just told Kevin she'd rather do this on her own. She felt uneasy about him using any kind of influence to get her an interview. And yet, he was hard to say no to. Especially when the thought of going out there and trying to find a job when she had no background information and work history was terrifying.

But this is it. This is the last thing I'm going to allow him to do for me. After this, I must solve my own problems.

* * *

That afternoon, Kevin walked into the office of Callahan Construction Company and plopped into the chair in front of Justine Carlucci's desk. Justine, who was working on the computer, turned and smiled. "Well, well. To what do we owe this rare pleasure?"

"Don't be snotty."

"*Moi?*"

"Yeah, *toi.*" But there were no teeth in Kevin's rejoinder. He and Justine had been friends for a long time. They understood each other. In fact, at one point he'd even thought about asking her out. But then he'd met Jill, and shortly afterward Justine had started dating Ange Carlucci. Last year she and Ange had been married. It was a second marriage for Justine, and everyone who knew her was happy for her.

Justine sobered and leaned back in her chair to regard him. "Seriously, what *does* bring you here? Patrick's in Whitley today, so if you came to see him, you're out of luck."

"I came to see you. I wanted to talk to you about Jane."

She frowned. "Jane?"

"The girl I found last week. I told you about her."

"Oh, yes. So she's regained her memory?"

"No, not yet."

"But you said her name was Jane."

"They had to call her something, so they named her Jane Doe in the hospital."

Justine nodded. "What about her?"

"Last week when I saw Patrick, he mentioned something about you needing help in the office."

"Yes, we've been running an ad in the paper, but so far, no luck."

"Jane needs a job, and I thought maybe—" Seeing the expression on her face, he stopped. "What?"

"Kevin, I don't think that's a good idea."

"Why not?"

"Well, for one thing, you don't know a thing about this girl. For another, I need someone who has some experience, someone I can trust."

"I know, but just talk to her, okay? If you don't feel good about her after that, fine. No harm, no foul."

"I don't know…"

"C'mon, Justine. Just talk to her. She really could use a break."

Justine sighed. "Have you mentioned this to Patrick?"

"No. You're the one who'll have to work with her. Besides, he'll go along with your decision, you know that."

She rolled her eyes. "Still the same old sweet-talker, aren't you?"

He grinned. "I try my best."

Her smile was resigned. "Oh, okay. I'll talk to her. But I'm not promising anything."

"I don't expect you to."

"The things I do for you," she grumbled.

He chuckled. "So how're the twins doing?"

"Driving me crazy."

"In addition to that."

"Isn't that enough?"

"They decide on a college yet?" Her girls, Monica and Melanie, were graduating from Rainbow's End High School in May.

"Monica has. She wants to go to UCLA." Justine rolled her eyes.

"Why so far away?"

"She says UCLA has the best film department of any college. She aspires to be a cinematographer. When I pointed out that one, we can't afford the out-of-state tuition and two, breaking into cinematography is about as easy as becoming president of the United States, she said I had a negative attitude."

Kevin laughed. "What does Ange say?"

"He says he's willing to pay for UCLA. Honestly, he'd give those girls anything they want, he's that crazy about them."

"What about Melanie?"

"I think Melanie is leaning toward A&M."

"Does she still want to be a vet?"

"Yes."

They talked awhile longer, then Kevin stood. "Thanks, Justine. I owe you."

"Damn right you do," she muttered as he leaned over to kiss her cheek.

"I'll take you and Ange out to dinner one night. Wherever you want to go."

"I'll settle for nothing less than the Rainbow's End Lodge."

"You got it. How *is* Ange, anyway?"

"Oh, you know Ange. Keeps saying he's going to lead a healthier lifestyle, but so far he hasn't done a thing to change."

Kevin gave her a sympathetic look. Justine's husband was a good bit older than her—in his early fifties compared to her forty—and his great passion was food. He was packing at least twenty extra pounds, and he hated to exercise...unless the exercise involved swinging a golf club. Kevin knew Justine worried about him. She'd told Kevin awhile back that it had taken her a long time to find Ange, and she didn't want to lose him. "We all have our vices," he said.

"Speak for yourself."

Kevin couldn't help laughing. He was still chuckling as he drove out of the parking lot and headed toward the women's center.

"Really? She's interested in talking to me?" Jane could hardly believe it.

"Don't look so surprised," Kevin said.

"But Kevin, I don't even know if I *have* any office skills."

"You told me you knew you could type."

"Yes, I...I can type." It was funny how that knowledge had come about, Jane thought. A couple of days ago, Margaret had been typing up the weekly schedule when she'd gotten a phone call. Jane had been in the office and when Margaret got up, something had drawn Jane to the keyboard. Almost as if she were in a trance, Jane sat down. Her fingers seemed to know exactly where to go, left on the keys A, S, D and F, the right ones on the keys J, K, L and the semicolon. Without conscious thought, she continued typing the schedule.

She even seemed to know the word-processing program Margaret was using.

When Margaret's phone call ended, she walked over and stood behind Jane, watching as she finished and saved the document.

"Well," she said with satisfaction, "looks like I've found myself a helper."

Jane looked up. She felt ridiculously happy. Such a small thing, discovering you knew how to do something, yet it gave her hope. If she remembered how to type, surely the rest of her life couldn't be far behind.

"Well then?" Kevin said now, pulling her back to the present.

"You twisted her arm, didn't you?"

"No. They need someone. I just suggested that you might fill the bill."

"You've done so much for me, Kevin. How will I ever repay you?"

"No payment is necessary. Anyway, what are friends for?"

His smile gave her a warm feeling, as if there really was someone who cared about her, no matter how alone she felt most of the time.

That evening he took her out for pizza and briefed her on the construction company and his family.

"Patrick's a good guy. Easy to work for. Easy to get along with," Kevin said. He took a large bite of his pizza. "You'll like him."

"What about Justine?"

"You'll like her, too. She's more reserved than Patrick, a little harder to get to know, but she's a really nice person."

Jane ate some of her own pizza. "I'm nervous," she admitted.

"That's normal."

"If only I…" She stopped. He was probably sick of hearing her whine.

"Will you quit worrying? Justine knows all about your situation, so you don't have to explain anything. Now c'mon, finish your pizza."

The following day, Jane dressed in the black skirt, green sweater and black flats she'd gotten at the center, carefully applied the lipstick and mascara she'd also been given and brushed her hair until it gleamed.

Kevin had apologized for not being able to take her to the interview, but he was expecting a furniture delivery at his new office, so Margaret arranged for a cab.

Jane liked Justine immediately. The older woman had an honest, no-nonsense look about her, with friendly hazel eyes and a quick, warm smile.

"This is awkward," she said once Jane was seated. "I usually have applicants fill out an application form, then we talk, but since you have no memory of your past…"

"I know," Jane said. "I realize you're only interviewing me because of Kevin."

"Kevin says you can type, though."

"Yes, it's weird how I know some things but have no clue about others. The doctor told me I might have islands of memory, and I guess that's what this is."

Justine leaned back in her chair and studied Jane thoughtfully. "Why don't you tell me what you *do* know."

"I seem to know the names of all the flowers I see. Verbena, lantana, plumbago, penta. And all the plants. And the birds."

"You like the outdoors."

"I seem to. I have this feeling that maybe I'm a gardener of some kind."

"What else?"

"Well…I also think I'm probably a good cook, because I have kitchen duty at the center this week, and I seem to instinctively know what to do. You know, how much salt to add to something, how to cook it, that kind of thing.'' Jane smiled ruefully. ''None of this would be very helpful in an office environment, I'm afraid.''

Justine regarded her for a long moment. Then she said, ''Jane, tell me this. Do you like people?''

''Yes, I do.''

''This job would require you to deal with our construction workers on a daily basis. And sometimes they can be a little crude. Think you could handle that?''

''I think I can.''

''If you worked here, you'd be doing a lot of the grunt work for me. Copying, filing, making coffee, some basic bookkeeping, mostly the stuff I don't have time for anymore. Not very exciting work, I'm afraid.''

''I'm not looking for excitement, Mrs. Carlucci.''

''Justine.''

Jane smiled. ''Justine. Like I said, I'm not looking for excitement. I just need a job. If you'll give me this one, I promise you I'll work very hard. You won't be sorry.''

''You know what, Jane? I don't think I will be, either. All right. If you want the job, it's yours.''

''Really?'' Jane could hardly believe it. She really hadn't expected Justine to hire her.

''Yes, but it may be a few days before you can start.''

"Oh." Jane couldn't help feeling disappointed.

"The problem is, I don't know how to handle the red tape. Since you don't know your identity, we have no social security number for you. I'm just not sure how we get around that."

"I didn't think of that." Of course they would need a social security number for her. Her heart sank. What if Justine found out she *couldn't* hire her? "Maybe I could get a new one?"

"Maybe. Let me check into it and I'll call you, okay? It might take a day or two."

"All right." Jane didn't know if she was a religious person or not, but as she waited for the cab that would take her back to the center, she found herself praying.

The Peck County Sheriff's Office was located in the municipal building on the square in downtown Rainbow's End. Kevin had decided to pay Sheriff Zach Tate a visit in person rather than telephoning, because he hadn't seen Zach in a while, and he liked him. He stopped on his way back from Austin.

Zach's secretary, Carol, looked up as Kevin entered the office. "Well, hi, Kevin."

"Hello, Carol."

They made small talk for a few minutes—Carol asking about his family and him asking about hers. Then she said, "Did you want to see Sheriff Tate?"

"Yes. I took a chance that he wouldn't be busy."

"You're in luck. He's working on the budget."

She grinned and said sotto voce, "He *hates* the budget." Still grinning, she picked up the phone and punched a button. "Sheriff Tate? Kevin Callahan is here to see you." She smiled at Kevin. "He says to go on in."

Zach Tate stood as Kevin entered his office. A good-looking man with the dark hair and eyes of his Cherokee ancestors, he was almost as tall as Kevin, who was an inch over six feet. The two shook hands, and Zach waved Kevin into one of the chairs flanking his desk.

"So what brings you here?" he said, leaning back in his chair and tenting his fingers.

"I was hoping you might be able to help me out."

Zach raised his eyebrows. "What's up?"

Kevin explained how he'd nearly run Jane down and everything that had transpired since. "So I was wondering if you could check and see if any young women hereabouts have been reported missing."

"Sure, that's no problem. I can do it right now. Everything's computerized, so it's easy."

He turned to his computer and began to type in commands. After a few minutes of studying the screen, he said, "You picked her up out on the highway between Pollero and Rainbow's End?"

"Yes."

"Too far from Austin to think she might have come from there." This was said more to himself than to Kevin. A few minutes later he shook his head. "Nothing. Only one missing persons report has been filed in the past week, and that's for a teenage boy who disappeared in Whitley."

Kevin hadn't realized how much he'd been hoping he could take Jane some information. "It's strange no one's missed her."

"Yeah, usually someone will. Even if there's no family nearby, there's usually a co-worker or a friend. You say you found her last Friday?"

"Yeah."

"So this is the sixth day."

Kevin nodded.

"I can make some calls. Check with the police in Austin and some of the other towns nearby. You never know what'll turn up."

Kevin knew by Zach's tone of voice that he didn't hold out much hope of finding out anything useful. "I'd appreciate that." He leaned back in his chair. "So how's married life treating you? You and Maggie still acting like newlyweds?"

The smile on Zach's face said it all. "She left for New York this morning. I miss her already."

Maggie owned a half interest in a literary agency in New York and visited the city every couple of months to meet with editors and other publishing professionals.

"How about you?" Zach said. "You doing okay?"

Kevin knew his cousin's husband was referring to Jill. "I'm fine," he said briskly.

Zach nodded. "Good."

That's what Kevin liked most about Zach. He never intruded into personal territory unless invited. Of course, Zach had had experience along those lines. His first wife had committed suicide when their youngest was just a baby. That had to have been hell. So he understood where Kevin was coming from.

"Well," Kevin said, getting up, "I'm not going to keep you. I know you're busy. Give Maggie my love, will you?"

"I will." He stood. "It was good to see you, Kevin."

They shook hands. Zach promised to call if he found out anything, and Kevin left.

As Kevin started for home, he wondered if Jane's interview was over. It was three o'clock, and she was supposed to meet with Justine at one.

He eyed his cell phone. He could call Justine. Or Jane. A few seconds went by. He picked up the phone. Then he put it back down.

He had to stop hovering over Jane. Besides, he could always call Justine.

Chapter Six

On Sunday afternoons, the Callahans traditionally gathered for dinner at the home of Rose and Patrick, Sr. In years past, when there weren't quite so many of them, Rose had done all the cooking herself. She still insisted on doing the main course and making her famous yeast rolls, but the younger women brought most of the side dishes and desserts.

Not everyone was there every Sunday, but the majority of the family came. Today was no exception.

Kevin had always enjoyed these family get-togethers, but the last year had been tough. Seeing his married siblings and their spouses and children had only emphasized the fact that Jill was gone and that he would not be joining their ranks.

But things were better lately. His family had settled down and stopped treating him as if he might go off the deep end, and Kevin himself had passed through the worst of the grief and pain and was finally beginning to feel like a human being again.

He arrived at his parents' home shortly after one. Almost everyone was already there, and those who weren't came within minutes of him. Soon the men were gathered around the TV set in the den where an Astros game was in progress. Kevin got himself a cold beer and joined them.

He could hear the women laughing and talking in the kitchen, along with the clink and clatter of dishes and pans and the giggles and noisy exuberance of the kids. All the normal Sunday sounds, he thought, smiling.

During the first commercial break after Kevin arrived, his brother Patrick turned to him and said, "Hey, Kev, that girl you referred to us is starting work tomorrow."

"Yes, she told me." Jane had called him on Friday. Her happiness at the job offer had made Kevin feel good.

"What girl?" his dad said.

Everyone looked at Kevin. "The girl I nearly ran down last week, Dad. You know. I told you about her."

"She's going to be working at the office?" Jack gave Kevin a pointed look.

"What's wrong with that?" Kevin knew what Jack was thinking, but dammit, there wasn't a thing wrong with him helping Jane get a job.

Jack shrugged. "Nothing. I was just surprised."

"She needed a job and I asked Justine to talk to her." Now everyone was looking at him. *"What?"* he finally said. "It's no big deal, is it?"

Was it Kevin's imagination or were they exchanging looks even as they mumbled things like "No" and "Nothing"?

The commercials ended, and soon their attention returned to the game, but Kevin still felt uncomfortable. What was wrong with him taking an interest in Jane? Any one of them would have done the same things he'd done. Hell, he was just being nice to someone who needed help.

But no matter how many times he told himself this, he knew he wasn't being entirely truthful with himself. Fact was, there was something about Jane that made him want to do things for her—more things than he might have done for anyone else in her situation.

Being with her, talking to her, helping her out, made him forget about himself, something that hadn't happened to him in a long time. And that felt good. He was tired of being poor Kevin, the guy everyone felt sorry for. With Jane he was someone else. She knew nothing about his background, nothing about Jill, so she didn't feel sorry for him. Just the opposite. To Jane, he was someone confident and strong, someone in charge of his life—the way he used to be before that life had changed so drastically. And Kevin liked having that feeling back. He liked having someone look to him for answers and strength.

Not long after this exchange, Keith's wife, Susan, came to the doorway of the den and announced that dinner was on the table.

Once the adults were settled around the dining room table—the children had their own table in the kitchen—Kevin's father said grace, then they started passing the food bowls. As always, there was an overabundance of food: today a huge ham, scalloped potatoes and potato salad, the yeast rolls, two salads as well as cole slaw, two kinds of beans, cooked cabbage, homemade apple sauce, a broccoli-rice-cheese casserole, and a corn soufflé that Patrick's wife Jan had made.

After everyone's plates were filled, the conversation picked up. The main topic on everyone's mind today was a controversial proposal by the mayor of Rainbow's End that the two main downtown streets be made into a pedestrian mall. The women were all for it, as was Kevin, who thought the aesthetics would far outweigh the inconvenience to motorists. Mostly his brothers were against the proposal, and a heated debate soon followed, with Sheila the most outspoken of either side.

When that debate died down—with no one winning anyone over to their point of view—Sheila grinned and tapped her water glass with her spoon. When everyone was quiet, she said, "Jack and I have an announcement."

"Not another baby," Rory said.

"Darn you, Rory," Sheila said. "I wanted to be the one to say the words. And, yes, that's our news." She smiled happily and looked at Jack. "We're thrilled to announce that another Kinsella baby will make his or her appearance in early October."

Kevin couldn't help a twinge of envy, but he congratulated Sheila and Jack just as everyone else did.

"So we're expanding our family yet again," Kevin's mother said. Her eyes were soft with love as she looked at Sheila. "I'm so happy for you and Jack, honey."

"Thank you, Mom."

After that, the conversation centered around the other grandchildren, with each parent giving updates on the news of the week.

Then, just as dessert—several varieties of pie— was being served, Jan, who was sitting on Kevin's left, said, "Patrick tells me that girl you found on the road outside of Pollero is going to start working at the office tomorrow."

"Yes."

"What's she like? Has she *really* lost her memory?"

"Yeah, she has."

"Gee, that must be tough," Susan said. "It was nice of you to befriend her, Kevin."

"So what *is* she like?" Jan persisted.

Before Kevin could answer, Sheila said, "She's very nice."

"Oh?" Jan said. "You've met her?"

"Uh-huh. Kevin brought her to our house for dinner last Saturday night."

"Really?" Jan said.

Now everyone was looking at him. Kevin shifted uncomfortably. Why were they making a federal case out of his friendship with Jane? "Hey, she's nice. I felt sorry for her." Immediately he wished he hadn't opened his mouth. He could see that instead of convincing them that he only had a passing, friendly interest in Jane, the same as he would if she had been a sixty-year-old woman or a twenty-year-old man, he had simply thrown fuel on the fire. He could see the women exchanging glances. Even his mother was giving him a speculative look. Looking for something, anything, that would sidetrack them, he said, "Glenn, will you pass me the sugar?"

"Sure." Glenn reached for the bowl.

"So, Kevin," Susan said, "do you know *anything* about this girl?"

Even though he knew showing any sign of irritation would be a mistake, he couldn't help himself. "No, I don't." He stirred his coffee. "Now, can we talk about something else?"

"Sorry," Susan said. But she didn't look sorry. She looked amused.

It was then Kevin decided that even if he did see Jane again, he would never let any member of his family know, because it was obvious they had the wrong idea about the relationship, and nothing he ever said was going to change their minds.

Justine had called Jane on Friday morning to tell her she could begin working for Callahan Construction Company on Monday. She even offered to pick Jane up at the center so she wouldn't have to worry about a ride. Jane was overjoyed, even as her happiness and excitement were tempered by concern that she wouldn't measure up to Justine's and Kevin's expectations.

Immediately after getting the call, Jane had headed for Margaret's office to tell her the news.

"That's wonderful, Jane," Margaret said. "And in the future don't worry about transportation. We have several volunteers who take our residents back and forth to their jobs, so you'll have a ride." She smiled. "Why don't you go to the clothing supply room and pick out a few more items? You'll need more clothes than you have if you're going to be working."

Jane spent a couple of hours in the supply room, which was constantly replenished by generous contributors, and was able to find two more pairs of neat slacks, several blouses and a denim skirt. She also found a blue cardigan sweater and a pair of brown leather clogs.

When she got back to her room, she debated whether or not to call Kevin. She finally decided he deserved to know how the interview had turned out, so she headed for the phones and placed the call. She got his voice mail and left him a message.

It was nearly nine that night when he called her back. He seemed really pleased to hear her news and told her he'd be looking forward to hearing how things went.

"I'm going out of town Monday morning and will probably be gone a couple of days, but I'll give you a call when I get back."

She was glad he didn't mention doing anything together over the weekend. It would have been hard to say no, because she felt so obligated to him. Maybe he was finally tired of looking after her and had come to the same conclusion she had, that he'd done enough for her and that it was time for her to begin to take care of herself.

For the rest of the weekend, she kept herself as busy as possible around the center. She found she enjoyed being around the children, so she volunteered to work in the nursery, which was in operation seven days a week as some of the residents had jobs that required weekend work.

A nondenominational service was held Sunday morning in a room that was designated the center's chapel, and Jane attended it with Wanda. She found the service—conducted by a minister from the United Methodist Church—to be soothing, and she left with a feeling of optimism and hope for the future.

That afternoon she played Scrabble in the recreation area with three of the women she'd met that first day—Dawn, the pregnant Lisa and Erin. She enjoyed herself more than she could have imagined she would only a few short days ago. Being with the women, listening to their stories, laughing at their jokes, was deeply satisfying. She wondered if, in her real life—the life she hoped she would soon remember—she had many women friends. She hoped so. She also wondered if many of these women stayed in touch with the others they met here at the center after they'd moved on. Somehow she had the feeling they probably didn't. Maybe being here was like being at camp when you were a kid. You thought you'd stay best friends with the girls you met there, but once you were home again, among your own circle of family and friends, those camp friendships eventually died a natural death.

Camp. Now where had that thought come from? Had she attended camp as a girl? She must have, otherwise how would she have known about camp friendships? Yet, no matter how hard she tried to bring up a specific memory, nothing surfaced.

Wanda owned a car and had invited Jane to go out for a hamburger with her that evening. Jane had thanked her but said since she had no money, she would have to decline. Wanda insisted it would be her treat and wouldn't take no for an answer, so at five o'clock, Jane left the Scrabble game and headed to her room to freshen up.

She enjoyed the outing with Wanda even though half her mind had already turned to thoughts of the next day and the job at Callahan Construction. That night, after they'd returned to the center, she found it hard to think of anything else.

She slept fitfully, and when the alarm went off at six o'clock, she was already awake. Eight o'clock found her dressed—denim skirt, white blouse and blue cardigan—and ready for Justine. When she saw Justine's dark-green Explorer pull into the parking lot, she grabbed her sack lunch, waved goodbye to the volunteer manning the reception desk and hurried out the door.

"Good morning," Justine said as Jane climbed up into the passenger seat.

"Good morning." Jane's heart was beating too fast with a mixture of excitement and trepidation. *Please, God, let me do a good job today.*

"I know you're probably nervous," Justine said as she expertly maneuvered the oversize vehicle into traffic, which was surprisingly heavy. "But don't be. We're a low-key office, and Patrick's a sweetheart to work for." She grinned. "Now when old man Callahan was in charge, it was a bit different."

"Old man Callahan? You mean Kevin's father?"

"Yes." Justine moved into the left-turn lane.

"Oh, don't get me wrong. Mr. Callahan wasn't an ogre or anything like that. He was just a stickler for doing things a certain way. Patrick's looser. He doesn't care how you do them, just so they're done." She eyed the sack lunch. "I see you brought your lunch. Good. I always bring mine, too. Saves a lot of money."

Jane smiled. She liked Justine a lot.

It took no time at all to get to the construction company. In fact, Jane thought it might even be possible to walk there from the center. She might try it one evening and see how long it took.

The parking lot was empty when they pulled in. "Patrick will be here at eight-thirty," Justine said.

Jane looked at her watch, which was the only piece of jewelry she'd had on when Kevin had found her. It was exactly eight-fifteen.

Inside, Justine turned on the overhead fluorescent lights and showed Jane the small kitchenette adjoining the office where there was a sink, a refrigerator, a microwave, a coffeemaker and a small table and two chairs. While Jane made coffee, Justine checked the answering machine for messages and booted up her computer.

By the time those things had been taken care of, the door opened and a Kevin clone walked in.

If Sheila's resemblance to her brother had been obvious, Patrick Callahan's was striking. The two men looked enough alike to be twins. Same body build, same height, same black hair, same brilliant-blue eyes. Wow, Jane thought. Those family genes were certainly strong. She'd known they were, from the portrait at Sheila's, but seeing the family resemblance in person was much more profound.

Justine introduced them, and Patrick gave Jane a warm smile. Even that smile was a twin to Kevin's.

"It's great to have you here," he said.

"Thank you. I'm happy to be here, too." She couldn't resist adding, "You certainly look a lot like Kevin."

"Yes," Patrick said, "people who don't know us always think we're twins. We're only two years apart."

Saying he needed to get some files ready for the accountant, he added, "I did tell you John was coming over this afternoon, didn't I?" Then he grabbed a cup of coffee and disappeared into his office.

For the rest of the morning Justine showed Jane the ropes. The time went by quickly. Before Jane knew it, it was noon and time for lunch. They ate it in the kitchen, then sat and talked for a little while before going back to work.

Like the morning, the afternoon seemed to fly by. Jane filed, she typed, she ran the copier, she sent faxes, she answered the phone, she met a few of the workers who came to the office about various matters—mostly insurance or worker's compensation questions—and was learning about the billing system when five o'clock rolled around.

"Well?" Justine said as they prepared to leave. "What do you think?"

"I think I'm going to love working here," Jane said.

"And I think I'm going to love having you. You're a good worker, Jane. You catch on quickly, and you work fast and don't make mistakes."

Jane felt as if someone had given her a million dollars. "Thank you."

That night Jane played Scrabble again with Wanda and two other women. By the time ten o'clock came, she was pleasantly tired and ready for bed. In the twenty minutes or so it took her to fall asleep she thought how different the center was from what she'd imagined when Kevin had first suggested she stay there. Instead of a cold, institutional feel, the center was more like a big commune—with everyone pitching in to do their share of the work and a real sense of camaraderie, almost like a big, extended family.

The only thing missing, she thought with a smile, were pets. Just as she drifted off to sleep, she decided that the first thing she'd do when she recovered her identity and a place of her own, would be to get a cat.

The next day was an even better one than Monday had been, because Jane felt more confident and was able to work without supervision for much of the time. She helped Justine with the accounts, both receivables and payables, and by the time five o'clock rolled around, Justine said she wasn't sure how she'd gotten along without her. Jane beamed at the praise.

On Wednesday Justine turned responsibility for all insurance-related problems, claims or questions over to Jane, saying it was a tremendous relief not to have to mess with them anymore. Jane read all the accompanying literature from their insurance carrier to familiarize herself with the policies and their terms, then she cleaned out the files and set up a new, more efficient system for dealing with claims. When she was finished, she kept looking at her neat labels. She knew she was probably grinning like a fool, but it felt wonderful to accomplish something completely on her own.

On Thursday Jane helped Justine get payroll ready. Justine explained that they'd tried to switch the pay system to twice a month, but had met with a lot of resistance from the majority of the men, who liked being paid at the end of every week.

"A lot of these guys can't hold on to their money very long, so getting paid every Friday is a godsend for them," Justine said. "It's only a nightmare for us here in the office."

"So all the men come here on Fridays to pick up their paychecks?" Jane asked. She'd already learned the company employed over two hundred workers.

"No. Only the crew supervisors come. Then they go back and distribute the paychecks to their men. I guess in the past when there weren't so many employees, they all used to come after work, but there are too many to do that now. We'd be here till seven or eight on Fridays if that were still the case.''

''How many supervisors are there?''

''Ten.'' Justine ticked them off. ''Patrick's brothers Keith, Rory and Glenn. Jack Kinsella, who's married to Patrick's sister.''

''Yes, I've met Jack.''

''Oh?'' Justine's eyebrows went up.

Suddenly Jane felt funny about saying how she'd met him, yet she could see Justine expected her to. ''I, um, Kevin took me to their house for dinner the day after he found me. I guess he felt sorry for me being alone and everything.''

''That was nice of him.'' Justine's expression was thoughtful.

''What about the other supervisors?'' Jane said.

''Oh, yeah. Okay, where was I? The others are Kenny Romero—he's a cutie—and Bobby Roeder, Ed Bassett, Rick Clemmons, Sam Roscoe, and Joe DiCarlo. I think that's ten. They're an interesting bunch.''

That night Kevin called. This was the first time Jane had heard from him since the previous Friday night. He explained that he'd been in Dallas meeting with a potential client.

''How'd the meeting go?''

''I think it went well. They seemed to like my ideas and preliminary design. I think I have a good shot at getting the job. If I do, it'll be my first commission.''

She could hear the pride in his voice and was happy for him. ''That's wonderful. What kind of a job is it?''

''A new office building that'll go up right here in Rainbow's End. The best part is, these guys have bought up nearly fifty acres, and this building will be just the first part of what they're planning. It could end up that I'd be designing not just this building but an entire office park as well as a group of cluster homes.''

''Cluster homes?''

''Kind of like town houses, only with no common walls. Usually the houses are built in clusters of four or six. They share a green area. What these guys are considering is a small park, with six units of cluster homes circling it.''

''This sounds like an ambitious project.''

''It is. But I didn't call to talk about me. How's the new job going?''

''It's going great.'' She told him some of what she'd been doing so far.

When she finished, he said, ''So you're really enjoying the job.''

''I am. And I can't thank you enough for helping me get it, Kevin.''

''Sounds to me like we're benefiting just as much as you are.''

Jane smiled.

''You'll be meeting the crew leaders tomorrow,'' he said.

''Yes, Justine told me.''

''Sometimes they can be a little crude. If they get out of line, just tell them to knock it off.''

''Don't worry. Justine warned me.''

''They don't mean anything by it, though. It's just that construction workers aren't used to being around women much, so they forget to watch their language when they are.''

''I understand. It won't be a problem.''

''It took Sheila a while to get used to their language, let me tell you.''

''Sheila?''

''Yeah, she used to work on one of the crews. In fact, Jack was her first supervisor.''

''Really? I can't picture her doing something like that.''

He laughed. ''That's because you don't know Sheila. She's stubborn and tough. Growing up with five brothers, she's had to be.''

''But construction…''

''I know. My dad felt the same way when she first told him that's what she wanted to do. See, she originally worked in the office. She had Justine's job. But she got sick of it. Sheila's an outdoor girl. She likes physical stuff. She was a real tomboy as a kid. Anyway, she threatened to leave Rainbow's End and go somewhere where she *could* get a construction job if Dad didn't let her work for him, so he caved. Sheila's my dad's only daughter. No way he was going to let her leave.''

Jane admired Sheila's determination. But it was still hard to picture Kevin's sister on a construction site. Sheila was so beautiful and so totally feminine.

''Were she and Jack a couple then?''

''No. But they got together soon after. I'll have to tell you about that sometime.''

''So how long did she work on a crew?''

''Less than a year.''

''What happened? Didn't she like it?''

''No, I think she liked it a lot. She quit because she was pregnant.''

They talked more, then Kevin said, ''I was wondering if you'd like to go into Austin with me on Saturday. I'll show you my new office and then we could have dinner there.''

Jane hesitated. It was so tempting to say yes, because it would be fun to spend the day with him and see his office. ''Thank you, Kevin, but I don't think...'' Her voice trailed off. What excuse could she give him?

''You don't think what?''

''I don't think I should.''

''Why not?''

''Kevin, I really appreciate everything you've done for me. You know that. But I can't keep leaning on you. I have to figure out how to get along on my own.''

''*Leaning* on me? It's just a drive into Austin.

Look, if you don't want to go, that's fine. You don't have to make excuses.''

Now she'd hurt his feelings. She took a deep breath. ''Kevin? If I ask you something, will you answer me honestly?''

''Of course.''

''Do you *really* want me to go? Or do you just feel sorry for me?''

Now it was his turn to hesitate. When he answered, the irritation she'd heard before was gone. ''Truth is, I kind of wanted to show off my office.''

Jane grinned. ''In that case, I'd like very much to go.''

Chapter Seven

Friday morning, Jane went to work with a keen sense of anticipation. She was looking forward to meeting all the crew leaders, especially Kevin's brothers Keith, Rory and Glenn. Justine had given her some background information on them, saying Keith was married but the other two weren't.

Jane tried to remember what Sheila had told her. "Keith is married to...Jan?"

Justine smiled. "No, Patrick is married to Jan."

Jane grimaced. "I'm glad I didn't say that in front of *him*, then."

"Oh, Patrick would have just laughed. He said sometimes it's hard for *him* to keep everyone straight." She sobered. "You'll meet Jan soon, I'm sure. She'll make it a point to stop into the office. She's a doll. You'll really like her. She volunteers at the center, you know.''

''Oh, that's right. I remember Kevin mentioning that. It's funny I haven't already met her.''

''Jan travels a lot. I know she was gone several days this week. She's a breast cancer survivor, and she has become a real advocate for early detection and prevention. She gives speeches all over the place now. I've never heard her talk, but Patrick says she's in great demand.'' Justine smiled. ''He's really proud of her.''

''You know, everyone in the Callahan family seems so nice.''

''They are. I feel fortunate to work for them.''

''Which one is Keith's wife?''

''That's Susan. She's the registrar at the local college. She's also really nice. And smart. She's just had her third promotion since she starting working there.''

''How old are the single brothers?''

''Rory is thirty-five, Glenn is thirty-two. Rory nearly got engaged last year, but it didn't work out. Glenn keeps saying he wants to get married, but as far as I know, he's never even been close.''

''And Kevin?'' Jane couldn't imagine why he wasn't married.

Justine sighed. ''Kevin's another story. He was engaged to a terrific girl, but just six weeks before their wedding, Jill was killed in an automobile accident on her way home from Dallas. She'd been visiting her parents. They were just devastated. She was an only child.''

''Oh, dear. How awful.''

''Yes. Keith took her death really hard. We were all worried about him. But lately he seems better. In fact, when he was in the other day to talk to me about you, he seemed almost like his old self. I hope so. He's a good guy.''

It made Jane feel bad to think about Kevin suffering like that.

Justine smiled wryly. ''I used to have a big crush on him.''

''Really?'' Somehow Jane couldn't picture the two of them together.

''But then he met Jill and I met Ange, and the rest is history.''

Soon after, they became engrossed in their work, and the subject of the Callahan brothers was dropped. The morning passed quickly, and about noon, the crew leaders began to stop by the office. The first one to show up was Jack, Sheila's husband. He gave Jane a friendly smile and asked how she liked working there.

''I love it.''

''Well, I know Justine's glad you're here.'' He grinned. ''Did she warn you about us?''

Jane laughed. ''Yes, and so did Kevin.''

''He ought to know.''

"Hey, Jack," Justine said, "Ange wants to know when you're going to give him another golf game."

Jack rolled his eyes. "Let's see. It'll be about fifteen years before the kids are grown and Sheila runs out of things for me to do on the weekends. Tell him I'll call him then."

Justine chuckled. "That bad, huh?"

"You don't know the half of it. Sheila's expecting another baby."

"Jack! *Really?*"

"Really. On second thought, tell Ange it might be twenty years before I'll have any time for myself."

Justine looked at Jane. "Don't let him kid you. He loves being married and having those kids to dote on. Those that hold out the longest fall the hardest, you know."

In answer, Jack pretended to swat at her.

After Jack, in quick succession came Ed Bassett, Rick Clemmons and Bobby Roeder. Jane wasn't crazy about Bobby, who kept staring at her breasts the whole time he was there.

When he'd gone, Justine said, "Sorry about that. Bobby's a pig, but he knows the construction business."

Around two o'clock, Keith and Rory Callahan showed up together. Once again Jane marveled at the strong family resemblance. What a good-looking bunch these Callahan brothers were.

"Glad to have you here," Keith said with a warm smile.

"I've really been looking forward to meeting you," Rory said.

Was it Jane's imagination or did he give her a funny look?

"Kevin told us about you," he explained. "He's taken a real interest in you."

"I owe Kevin more than I can ever repay," she said self-consciously.

"Kev's a good guy," Rory said.

While they were talking, another man walked in. Jane immediately knew he wasn't a Callahan, although he was every bit as good-looking, with thick, dark hair and very dark eyes.

"Hey, Kenny, how're you doing?" Keith said.

"Great," the man said.

Jane figured this must be Kenny Romero.

"Your crew's working on that Pollero apartment project, right?" Rory asked.

"Yeah, that's us," Kenny said.

"How's it going?" Keith asked.

"We're ahead of schedule."

"That'll make Patrick happy," Rory said.

"Kenny," Justine said, "this is my new assistant, Jane."

"Hey, Jane, nice to meet you."

"Thanks."

After a few minutes of talking among themselves, the men collected their crews' paychecks and left.

"That only leaves Joe DiCarlo, Glenn and Sam Roscoe," Justine said. "And they'll be here soon. Usually everything has been picked up by three because the crews pretty much knock off at four o'clock on Fridays."

A few minutes later Justine looked up from her computer and said, "Here comes Sam. That's his black pickup that just pulled into the parking lot."

Jane was standing at the filing cabinet and had her back to the door. She didn't turn around until she heard it open. She took one look at the big, sandy-haired man who entered and her heart knocked painfully against her chest. She stared at him, fear nearly paralyzing her.

"Jane? Jane, what is it?" Justine said.

"I...I—" *Jonathan,* she thought, beginning to shake. Her head spun as her memory came rushing back. Her legs would no longer support her, and she sat down heavily.

"What's wrong?" the blond man said.

Annie stared at him, her heart pounding, but as realization slowly dawned, bringing with it the knowledge that this man wasn't Jonathan as she'd first thought, her heart calmed and she was able to breathe again.

There *were* superficial resemblances between them—their body builds were the same and they both had streaked, light-brown hair. So she could see why, in that initial moment when she'd first seen this man backlit in the doorway, she had thought he was Jonathan. She swallowed. Thank God he wasn't.

"Are you okay?" Justine asked softly, kneeling in front of Annie.

Annie nodded. Her head was still spinning.

"What happened?"

Annie's gaze darted to the blond man. "He..." She took a deep breath. "He resembles my ex-husband," she said in a firmer voice.

For a moment Justine looked at her blankly. Then, her face breaking into a smile, she said, "Your *memory's* back?"

Annie slowly returned the smile. "It seems to be."

Justine sat back on her haunches. "Well." She looked up at the man. "Sam, you did good."

He looked confused. "I'm glad. I guess."

"Jane here..." Justine stopped. "But I guess your name isn't Jane, is it?"

"No," Annie said. "It's...Annie. Annie... Alcott."

"Well, Annie Alcott, meet Sam Roscoe, another of our crew leaders. Sam, Annie's my new assistant. She's had amnesia, and seeing you seems to have brought her memory back."

Annie stood up and stuck her hand out. "I'm very happy to meet you, Sam. And grateful to you, too."

He grinned as they shook. "Glad to be of service." Turning to Justine, he said, "I'll just get my guys' checks and get out of your way."

A few minutes later he was gone.

Now that her fear had subsided, Annie felt euphoric. Even though the return of her memory had renewed her fear she would never be free of Jonathan, she was thrilled to have a name, an identity and a history. To know that she wasn't destitute or a criminal, as she had sometimes secretly feared.

She smiled, remembering her apartment and her car and her bank account, which had a healthy balance. Then her smile faded. Her apartment. Yes, she remembered it, but she didn't remember leaving it. She tried to think, but the last thing her mind could conjure was opening the door to Jonathan and their subsequent confrontation.

She must have looked dazed, because Justine said, "Are you okay, Annie?"

Annie nodded slowly. "Yes, but I just realized…it's been two weeks since Kevin found me. I don't know what's happened to my apartment, if I locked the door when I left…or anything."

She bit her lip. She knew she wasn't making any sense. How could she have locked the door? She hadn't had any keys on her when Kevin found her.

As suddenly as it had come, her euphoria evaporated, and tears filled her eyes. Immediately she was ashamed of herself. "I—I'm sorry."

"Don't apologize. You've had a shock. It's no wonder you're upset." Justine looked around. "Darn. I wish Patrick was here. If he was, I'd take you on home. Give you some time to get your bearings."

Annie fought to calm herself again. Despite Justine's kindness, there was no reason for her to get upset. Her memory had returned. Everything else would get sorted out. "Don't worry about me," she said in a stronger voice. "I'll be okay. I don't need to go home."

The words were barely out of her mouth when the door opened and another of the men walked in. Annie knew without being told that this was Kevin's youngest brother, Glenn. Once again that family resemblance couldn't be denied.

"Glenn," Justine said in obvious relief. "Am I glad to see you."

He grinned. "I haven't had that nice a reaction from a good-looking woman in a while."

"Would you mind staying for about fifteen minutes while I run Annie home?" Justine said. "Joe DiCarlo hasn't picked up his checks yet, or I'd just lock up and go."

"Sure, no problem." He looked at Annie curiously.

Justine introduced them, told Glenn what had just happened, refused to listen to Annie's protestations that she was fine and, after thanking Glenn again, hurried Annie out the door.

"Now when you get back to the center, you tell the director everything, and they'll help you."

Annie nodded gratefully. Although she'd told Justine she was fine and could have stayed at work for the rest of the afternoon, she was glad Justine hadn't listened. "Thank you. You've been...*everyone's* been so kind."

"Remember what I told you," Justine said when she pulled into the center's parking lot. "Tell the director everything. They'll know exactly what to do to get things straightened out for you."

Annie thanked Justine again. She really wanted to call Kevin, but she knew she had to stop depending on him. Besides, she was going to see him tomorrow. She could tell him everything then.

So when she got inside, she headed straight for Margaret's office. It was empty. "Where's Margaret?" she asked the volunteer who was using the copy machine.

"Her sister's little girl had an accident at school, so Margaret went over to watch the baby while her sister went to the hospital," the volunteer said. "Can I help you?"

"No. No, I need to see Margaret. Do you know when she'll be back?"

The volunteer shrugged. "If it's really important, I can page her."

Annie shook her head. "It's okay. I'll just leave her a note."

Disappointment caused her shoulders to sag. She had so hoped someone would be able to take her to Pollero tonight so she could check on her apartment and her car. Now she would have to wait until to-morrow. She sighed. Well, it couldn't be helped.

Then she brightened. Aunt Deena! She had a family! And a beloved aunt! Maybe she wouldn't be able to go to Pollero tonight, but she *could* call her aunt, who was probably worried since she hadn't heard from her last week.

Feeling a lot better, Annie headed for the phones. It was wonderful to know that she had someone to worry about her.

The phone was ringing when Kevin walked into the house, but by the time he answered, the caller had hung up. Caller ID showed the number of the construction company office, so he called there.

"Kevin?" Justine said. "Oh, good. I was hoping to talk to you this afternoon."

Kevin listened quietly as Justine told him what had happened earlier. "So she remembered everything?"

"Apparently. But she's upset, so I took her back to the center. Thing is, in the excitement, I forgot to give her her paycheck. And I can't leave here again."

"I'll come and get it."

"I was hoping you'd say that. I think she needs someone to talk to right now, and she trusts you more than anyone."

Twenty minutes later Kevin, armed with Jane's—

no, he had to quit thinking of her as Jane—armed with *Annie's* paycheck, was on his way to the center.

When he got there, he could hardly wait for Annie to come out. He paced up and down until he heard the inner door open. Her face lit up when she saw him, the first time he'd seen her look truly happy since he'd found her.

"I brought your paycheck," he said.

"Oh, thank you. I forgot all about it."

"Yes, Justine told me."

"She explained what happened?"

"Yes. She called me. She felt bad about forgetting to give you your check, plus she thought maybe you'd be anxious to talk."

"I am. In fact, I almost called you."

"Why *didn't* you?"

"Well, I figured I was going to see you tomorrow. I didn't want to bother you."

"Jane, it's—" He broke off. "Sorry. It's going to take a while before I'm used to calling you Annie."

She grinned. "It's okay."

"Anyway, like I started to say, you're not a bother. I don't know where you got that idea." It frustrated him that she couldn't seem to realize he *liked* helping her.

"Thank you."

"Justine also told me you're worried about your apartment."

She nodded. "I was hoping Margaret would find

someone to take me there tonight, but she's not here, so I guess it'll have to wait until tomorrow morning."

"Where is your apartment?"

"Pollero."

"I can take you."

"You can?"

"Sure. You ready to go now?"

"I'd love to go now. But are you sure it's not too much trouble?"

"I was the one who offered, wasn't I?" he said patiently.

"Yes." Her smile was sheepish. "But it *can* wait until tomorrow. In fact, if you'd like to just stop there before we go into Austin tomorrow, that would be fine, too."

"I'm going to my nephew's baseball game tomorrow morning. Let's do it now. It's not a problem."

"Okay."

She signed out, and once they were in his truck, he said, "Okay. Tell me everything." His jaw tightened as she explained what had happened to her earlier on the day he'd found her.

"You mean your ex-husband *hit* you?" Why, that son of a bitch. Kevin had no use for men who beat up on women.

"He...I don't think he meant to. The thing is, he's never accepted the divorce."

Kevin looked at her. He couldn't believe she was

making excuses for that scumbag. "How long have you been divorced?"

"A year."

"That's plenty of time for him to have adjusted. There's no excuse for him hitting you."

"I know how it sounds, but Jonathan isn't really a bad guy. He just..." She sighed. "It's hard to explain."

"Has he hit you before that day I found you?"

She didn't answer for a moment. Finally she said, "Yes," in a small voice.

Kevin felt like hitting something himself, preferably her ex-husband's face. "How long did it go on before you left him?"

"The first time he hit me was about two years ago."

Kevin had read about women who stayed in abusive relationships, but he'd never understood why. Maybe if the women involved were uneducated or unsophisticated, but Annie didn't seem to fall in either category. Kevin tried to imagine his sister or, for that matter, *any* of the women he knew putting up with that kind of behavior, and he couldn't. Why, Sheila would probably deck the guy herself if anyone tried anything like that with her. Even his mother, who belonged to a different generation, would never allow herself to be a punching bag.

"Why'd you stay with him?" he said.

Another deep sigh. "It's a long story."

"I don't have anywhere else to go."

"To understand about my marriage, I have to tell you how I grew up."

"I'm listening."

"I grew up in the northeast—the Boston area. I was a surprise baby, born when my sister—who's my only sibling—was ten years old. My mother didn't want another child. She had gone back to school and gotten her Ph.D. in English and was teaching at the university. She didn't have any interest in another baby. In fact, I've always been surprised she didn't just have an abortion. Instead she hired a succession of nannies and continued with her life as if I wasn't there."

Her voice was so matter-of-fact, and yet Kevin knew the hurt ran deep. He thought back to his own childhood. How his earliest memories of his mother were her hugs and kisses. How he would run home from school to show her his latest drawings or grades. How no matter how busy she was or what she was doing, she always stopped and listened and praised. How every day she told her children how much she loved them.

"I was a lonely kid," Annie continued. "My father was a lot older than my mother—almost twenty years—and a scientist. He worked long hours and when he was home, he spent most of his time in his laboratory there. He loved me, I think, but he didn't know how to show it."

"What about your sister?"

Annie shrugged. "Emily was similar to our father, more involved in science and studying than in people. She's an archaeologist. She and her husband are in Peru right now. Have been for the past couple of years. I rarely see her. We haven't even talked on the phone for six months.

"Anyway, my father died of cancer when I was twelve. He was sixty-seven. Less than a year later my mother remarried. That marriage only lasted two years. Six months after the divorce, she married for the third time. She met Ian, her current husband, at the university. He was a visiting professor from England. When I was sixteen, they moved to London."

"*They* moved to London? What about you?"

"By then I'd been in boarding school for two years, and my mother felt that was the best place for me to stay."

"Where was your sister?"

"She was in graduate school."

Kevin knew there were families like hers, but he'd never known any. He couldn't imagine being left like that.

"I wasn't completely alone," she said, as if she knew what he was thinking. "I have a great-aunt I'm close to, and I spent my holidays and vacations with her. She's a wonderful person. Still, I was very vulnerable to someone like Jonathan.

"I met him my first year of college. I went to Harvard. He'd graduated from Harvard Medical School and was just completing his residency at Boston General. He's nine years older than me."

"How'd you happen to meet?"

"It was one of those strange things that happen sometimes. I went to the hospital to visit my roommate who'd broken her leg skiing. Jonathan got on the same elevator. The elevator got stuck between floors. He and I were trapped there for more than three hours before they could get us out."

"Just the two of you?"

"Yes. By the time we were rescued, he'd asked me out. I really didn't stand a chance against him. I'd been looking for love and attention all my life, and he gave it to me. He was so charming, so handsome. He literally swept me off my feet. I married him three months later. At the end of his residency, when he was offered a place on staff at the medical center in Austin, we moved to Texas."

Kevin listened without comment as she went on to describe her marriage. How Jonathan seemed so wonderful at first. How his attentiveness and concern were so welcome to her, how he made her feel so loved and special.

But how, over the years, as she matured, she began to chafe at his possessiveness and jealousy. How he wouldn't let her work. How he didn't want her to go back to school. How he controlled what she wore, what she did, even what she ate.

How, when she disagreed with him or tried to assert herself in any way, he became more and more abusive. How desperately she had wanted children and how she despaired when she couldn't conceive, only to discover that, unbeknownst to her, Jonathan had had a vasectomy.

"When I confronted him about the vasectomy and accused him of lying to me, he became enraged. It scared me, the way he shouted that he would never share me with anyone else. At first I backed off. I kept telling myself how good he was, how much he'd done for me, how much he loved me. And then he hit me. I was so shocked, I almost persuaded myself it hadn't happened. And he was so sorry afterward. He cried. He said he didn't know what had come over him. He was so solicitous, so loving. He kept saying he loved me so much, and he would never, ever hurt me intentionally. I believed him. I honestly thought it was my fault, that I'd provoked him.

"For a while after that, everything was wonderful, almost as wonderful as it had been when we'd first married. He stopped bugging me about everything, and I began to think he'd changed. That hitting me had been as much of a shock to him as it had been to me, and that now our marriage was going to be different.

"Of course, it wasn't. Little by little, we fell into the same patterns. And then the day came when he hit me again. Only this time, it wasn't just once. This time he really hurt me.

"So I left him. But he wouldn't leave me alone. He kept coming to my apartment. Following me. Calling me. Begging me to come back to him, even after the divorce was final. And then threatening me when I refused. It was awful. I got so I was jumpy all the time. When he started phoning me at work, I knew I had to move away, out of his sphere, if I ever hoped to build a new life and have any peace at all.''

She told Kevin she'd chosen Pollero because it was small and off the beaten track and she didn't think Jonathan would find her there. ''But I was wrong. Somehow he tracked me down.''

''Why did you let him in?'' This question had been on Kevin's mind ever since she first told him what had happened.

Annie sighed. ''I felt sorry for him. He looked terrible. He said he just wanted to talk to me. He said he'd changed. That he'd get counseling. He said he loved me so much, that he couldn't bear to live without me. He even said he'd have his vasectomy reversed and we could have children.

''I tried to be as gentle as possible. But I told him I just couldn't. That I didn't love him anymore.''

''And then he got furious and beat you. What I want to know is why you haven't reported him to the police?''

''Oh, Kevin, I can't do that. I don't want to ruin his life. He's a wonderful doctor. People look up to him. And it isn't as if he'd been beating me for years or anything. It was just those couple of times.''

Kevin swore. ''Just those couple of times! Listen to yourself. He doesn't deserve your sympathy.''

"Look, I know what you're saying. But I just want to forget the past. Besides, I think he's finally faced that it's really over now. And I don't think he'll bother me again."

Chapter Eight

Annie knew by Kevin's disapproving silence that he wanted to argue with her, and she was grateful that he didn't. Maybe he was right. Maybe she should have reported Jonathan.

She thought about the women she'd met at the center. About how many of them had come from abusive relationships. But she wasn't like them. She hadn't allowed Jonathan to beat her for years the way some of them had.

Yes, she'd excused that first time, because she really had thought it was an aberration on his part and would never happen again. But when it did, she'd left him.

And this last time, well, it really *was* the last time,

because now Jonathan knew that no matter what he did or said, she wasn't coming back to him. That's why he'd been so enraged. Because she had finally made her position so clear he couldn't deny it.

But even as she told herself this, she couldn't get rid of a last remnant of doubt. Because when had Jonathan *ever* given up? On anything?

"Okay," Kevin said. "Here we are on Huffman Road. Where are the apartments?"

Annie shook away her gloomy thoughts. Time enough later to figure out what action she needed to take, if any. She pointed. "Turn right at that stop sign. After you turn, the apartments will be about half a mile down, on the left. They're called Country Garden Apartments. Mine is number eighteen."

He followed her directions, and when they reached the apartment entrance, she showed him where to park. She looked around nervously as they got out of his truck. It wasn't that she really expected Jonathan to be lying in wait; it was just that she'd been nervous for such a long time, it was hard to break the habit.

She breathed a sigh of relief as she saw that there was no one lurking about, certainly no black BMWs in the parking area, which was what Jonathan drove. She was also relieved to see that the front door to her apartment was closed. She'd been afraid it might be standing wide-open. When they tried the door, they found it was also locked.

"Let's go around back," she said. "See if that

door's locked.'' As they approached the back of her apartment, she saw her car parked in her slot. She smiled. It would be great to have a car at her disposal again.

Kevin walked to the door. "It's locked, too. Do you think you locked up when you left?"

"I don't know. I don't remember. I didn't have any keys on me when you found me, did I?"

"No."

"The locks are dead bolts. They couldn't have been locked without one."

He nodded, looking around. "Is there a manager on site?"

"Yes."

"Let's go see him."

She smiled. "It's a her."

"Okay. Let's go see her."

They were in luck. The manager was in her office, although she was standing behind her desk, gathering up papers, and looked as if she was preparing to leave when they walked in. "Yes?" She looked up. "May I help you?"

"Mrs. Rosen?" Annie said. "You don't remember me, do you? Annie Alcott? I rented number eighteen about three weeks ago."

Susan Rosen peered at Annie over her glasses. "Actually, I do remember you. For a moment there, I just didn't recognize you. Well, I'm certainly glad to see you. I wondered where you were. And your husband's been *very* worried."

Annie's heart sank. "My husband?"

"Yes. He's called and come by here at least half a dozen times in the past two weeks. I *told* him if he was *that* worried, he should call the cops. But he said he didn't want to do that, because you had a history of taking off and that he was sure you'd turn up soon."

Before Annie could answer, Kevin said, "That man is her ex-husband, and he's been stalking her. That's why she left."

"You know, I wondered. There was something about him that bothered me. Well, if that's the case, when he comes back, I won't tell him anything."

"Did he say he was coming back?" Annie asked. *Of course he'll come back. You always knew that, didn't you? You were just pretending before, trying to reassure yourself, but he'll never leave you alone. Never.*

"When you left, you left your doors unlocked," Susan Rosen said. "I locked them, though. I didn't want anyone going in there who didn't belong. I figured that's what you'd want."

"Thank you," Annie said. Her heart was beating too hard. Suddenly she was terrified Jonathan would show up before they could get away. "Can you let us into the apartment? I...when I left, I left my keys inside. See, I fell and hurt myself and I guess I wandered out. I—" She stopped. She knew she was hardly making sense.

"Look," Kevin said, "the truth is, her ex-husband barged his way into her apartment and when she refused to go back to him, he hit her and knocked her out. When she came to, she was dazed and didn't remember who she was or where she was and she wandered out. That's why the doors weren't locked. She just got her memory back today. She wants to check the apartment and would appreciate you opening it up for her.''

"Certainly," Susan Rosen said. "You know, the telephone installer is the one who told me you weren't there and the apartment was wide-open.''

Annie remembered how she'd been waiting on the installer when Jonathan had arrived that day.

Susan Rosen opened a drawer, rummaged through its contents for a few seconds, then lifted out a key. "This is it.''

They followed her to the apartment, where she unlocked the door and let them in. Annie walked straight back to the kitchen. Her purse and the groceries she'd brought home that day were still sitting there, as was her umbrella. She hurriedly looked through her purse. Her keys, driver's license, checkbook and credit cards were all there.

"So you're all set?" Susan Rosen said.

"I think so."

"All right. If there's anything else I can do, just let me know."

"Just don't tell my ex-husband anything."

"Oh, I won't, believe me."

"He can be very persuasive."

"I've dealt with guys like him before. I can't be intimidated by them."

Annie nodded. "Good. I'll give you a call in a few days. In the meantime can you figure out what it will cost me to get out of my lease? I can't stay here now. He'd never give me any peace."

"Are you sure you want to let him drive you out?" Susan Rosen said. "You could get a restraining order against him."

"A restraining order wouldn't work. I've tried that before. He doesn't pay any attention."

"Okay. I'll see what I can do about the lease."

"Thank you."

After Susan Rosen left, Kevin said, "I'm glad you're not going to stay here." He smiled. "What do you want to do first?"

"Throw out the spoiled food." She held her nose as she lifted out a package of ground meat and a carton of milk.

They made short work of the groceries, then Kevin said, "What else?"

"Will you help me pack up some things and load them into my car? I want to take my car back to the center with me."

"Let's get busy, then."

It took about an hour for them to pack up her clothes and personal belongings. When Kevin said there was plenty of room for more in the bed of his truck, Annie decided she would love to take her aunt Deena's rocking chair, too, so he loaded that up.

Annie felt a twinge of sadness as they locked up and left. She had loved this apartment, and she'd had so little time to enjoy it. Damn Jonathan! Why couldn't he just accept reality?

When they got back to the center, Kevin helped her unload everything and get it into her room. When they were finished, he said, "I'm starving. Why don't we go and get something to eat?"

Annie hesitated. It was tempting to just say okay. But she needed to be sure Kevin wasn't asking her out of a misguided sense of duty. She especially didn't want him feeling sorry for her. So she said, "Look, Kevin, I appreciate everything you did for me tonight. But you don't have to worry about me. I mean, you're taking me out tomorrow, and I'm sure you must have other things to do tonight."

"If I had something else to do, I wouldn't have asked you to come and eat with me."

"Are you sure?"

"What do I have to do? Toss you over my shoulder and carry you off?"

She laughed. "All right, all right, I get the point. In that case, do you mind waiting a few minutes? I want to change clothes."

"Why? You look fine the way you are."

"Thanks, but I've been wearing borrowed clothes for weeks. I think I'll feel more like me in my own things."

"Okay. I'll wait outside."

While Kevin waited, he thought about everything

he'd learned today. He was glad Annie had recovered her memory and that she was going to continue to be cautious where her former husband was concerned, but he didn't agree with her decision not to tell the police about this latest beating. That jerk didn't deserve any consideration from her. No man who hit women did.

He was still thinking about her situation when, ten minutes later, she emerged from the center and walked over to the truck.

He smiled at the picture she made. She looked nothing like the dazed, fragile girl he'd rescued only two weeks ago. Today she walked confidently, and there was a smile on her face.

She'd changed into cargo pants and a scoop-necked red T-shirt. Both fit her snugly and showed off her slim, curvy figure. And she'd done something different to her hair, pulling the sides back from her face and securing them on top of her head with a silver clip. Dangling silver earrings sparkled and swung free as she walked toward him.

For the first time since he'd found her, Kevin was struck by the fact that not only was Annie pretty, she was also sexy. The realization rattled him, because it was the first time since Jill died that he'd consciously thought of another woman in that context.

Unsettled, he got out of the truck and walked around to open the passenger door for her. As he helped Annie into the cab, he was very aware of her—the warmth of her body, her slim, lightly tanned arms, the fresh, flowery fragrance she wore, the way her hair shimmered in the afternoon sunlight. It was as if all his senses had suddenly awakened after a long hibernation. But even as his body responded to the living, breathing woman with him, his heart ached from the knowledge that the woman he'd loved so much was already fading from his memory. *I'm sorry, Jill. I'm so sorry.*

As he walked back to the driver's side of the truck, he told himself there was nothing to feel sorry about. Jill would be the last person to expect or want him to go the rest of his life without being attracted to another woman. What he was feeling was normal. He couldn't expect to remain frozen forever.

If the shoe were on the other foot—if it had been him to die and Jill to live, wouldn't he want her to find someone else? Of course he would. He'd loved her. He would never want her to be unhappy or feel guilty because she was attracted to another man.

Annie smiled at him when he climbed in beside her.

He cleared his throat. Forced his thoughts to focus on the present and not the past. This was Annie's night, and he didn't want to spoil it for her. "What do you feel like eating?"

"I'm not picky. Whatever you want is fine with me."

"I'm leaning toward Mexican. Do you like Mexican?"

"I love it."

"Okay, I'll take you to my favorite place, then. Rosa's Cantina. They have the best enchiladas and fajitas in town. Not to mention margaritas to kill for."

"I haven't had a margarita in months."

"Then you can live it up tonight. Besides, you've got something to celebrate. Your memory's back."

"I know. It feels wonderful, too."

Fifteen minutes later they were settled across from one another in a booth in the popular restaurant, which was already almost full, and it wasn't even six o'clock yet. Kevin knew by seven there would be people waiting for tables. Friday nights were the most popular night to eat out in Rainbow's End. They'd barely gotten settled in their seats when their waitress—Rosa's daughter Sylvia—brought them a basket of warm chips and a bowl of salsa.

"Hello, Kevin." She gave him one of her flirty smiles. "Haven't seen you here lately."

"Hello, Sylvia. How you doin'? How's school?"

"Next semester I do my student teaching. Then, in December, I graduate." She grinned. "I can't wait."

"That's great. Sylvia, this is Annie, a friend of mine. Annie, this is Rosa's daughter, Sylvia Cardenas."

"Hi," Annie said. "It's nice to meet you."

"You, too," Sylvia said. She eyed Annie speculatively. "You new in town? I don't think I've seen you around before."

"Yes, I'm new."

Kevin knew Sylvia was curious about Annie, but she was too polite to ask any more questions. "Annie's working for the construction company."

Sylvia nodded. "Well, it's nice to have you here." Turning to Kevin, she said, "What can I get for you to drink?"

They placed their drink orders, then studied their menus.

"Which of the enchilada dishes are the best?" Annie asked.

"I like the enchilada platter, because you get some of everything, but it's a lot to eat."

"I think I'll just order the spinach enchiladas."

"That's a good choice."

After Sylvia brought their drinks and took their order, Kevin leaned back and studied Annie. "You look different tonight."

"Do I?"

He nodded. "Maybe it's because you're wearing your own clothes, or maybe it's because you finally know who you are, but you seem more sure of yourself."

"I feel more sure of myself." She made a face. "And if it wasn't for being afraid Jonathan might find me again, I'd say I feel better than I ever have."

Kevin's jaw clenched. "If he so much as gets within ten feet of you, all you have to do is call me or Zach Tate. In fact, I really think you should talk to Zach. Let him know what's going on with your ex. He could go put the fear of God into him.''

She shook her head. "I told you, I don't want to make trouble for him. And maybe I'm worrying for nothing. Maybe the only reason Jonathan came to the apartment so many times is he really *was* worried about me. Maybe he felt terrible about hitting me and wanted to make sure I was all right.''

"Why'd he lie to the manager, then?''

"He couldn't very well admit to her that he'd hit me.''

"No, but I still think—''

She put her hand up. "I know, but I don't want to talk about Jonathan, anymore, okay? I just want to have fun tonight. To celebrate, like you said.''

Reminding himself that he'd already decided he wasn't going to rain on her parade—at least not tonight—Kevin let the subject of her ex drop.

From then on, they drank their margaritas, ate chips, then enjoyed their dinners.

Despite his determination to make the evening a good one for Annie, Kevin was not entirely comfortable. He was too aware of the difference in his feelings toward her, which were only intensified by the fact she seemed to grow prettier by the minute. He couldn't believe he hadn't realized how attractive she was before now. He really *had* been asleep, he thought ruefully.

By the time the evening had come to an end, he

knew he had some hard thinking to do. And uppermost on that list of things to think about was Annie and what role, if any, she was going to play in his future.

Because if what he was feeling tonight was just a normal, physical reaction he might have felt for any reasonably attractive woman at this stage of his recovery from Jill's death, then he needed to be careful. The last thing he wanted to do was give Annie the wrong impression or hurt her in any way.

She'd been hurt enough.

They didn't talk much on the way home, and Annie was glad. Her mind felt as if it were on overload, so much had happened to her today. She knew it would be hard to sleep tonight.

It didn't take long to reach the women's center. Less than fifteen minutes after leaving Rosa's, Kevin pulled into the parking lot and cut the engine.

He looked over at Annie. His eyes gleamed in the darkened cab. "Thanks for coming with me tonight. I enjoyed it."

"Thanks for *asking* me." She'd had a wonderful time, the best time she could remember having in years.

"Still feel like going to Austin with me tomorrow?"

"You know, I've been thinking about that. It might not be a good idea for me to be seen in the city."

"Why not?"

"Because I lived there for a long time. I have a lot of friends there, and so does Jonathan. I don't think I should take a chance on running into any of them."

"I didn't think of that."

"I'm sorry, Kevin. I'd love to go, but I better not." She picked up her purse and reached for the door handle.

"Don't worry about it. It's okay. And wait...I'll get the door for you." He got out and walked to her side of the truck, opened her door and reached for her hand. As his warm fingers closed around hers, Annie's hand tingled.

For a long moment after she stepped down, neither moved. They were standing so close together that she could feel the warmth of his body, even though they weren't touching. As their eyes met and clung, she was very aware of her body. She could almost see the blood running through her veins, her heart beating, her breath quickening.

She swallowed.

He was going to kiss her.

Instinctively she leaned closer.

Time seemed suspended as around them the world moved on. Annie heard the hum of traffic, a mockingbird's call, the rustle of leaves as a nearby tree was buffeted by a gust of wind, the sound of a car approaching on the roadway beyond. But they didn't seem real. The only reality was Kevin...and the kiss....

The car passing by backfired.

She jumped. Blinked. What was she doing? She took a step backward. "I...thanks again, Kevin," she said all in a rush. "I had a great time. I—I'd better go in. I'm really tired." She knew she was babbling, probably not making any sense at all, but she was so frightened by what she'd nearly done, she couldn't think straight.

"Of course," he said.

She heard the puzzlement in his voice. Oh, God, now she'd hurt his feelings. He probably thought she was repulsed by him. She wanted to touch his face, to say how sorry she was, that her withdrawal had nothing to do with him personally, that she might look okay, but inside she was a jumble of fears and uncertainties.

"Good night, then, Annie."

She prayed for him to say he'd call her, but he didn't. Not knowing what else to do, she said good-night and headed for the front door. Before she went in, she stopped and waved, and he waved back. Then he started the truck and drove away.

Heart heavy, Annie went inside. What a mess she'd made of things.

"Hey, Jane, you look nice. I missed you at dinner."

Annie had been so lost in her thoughts she hadn't even seen Wanda, who was coming out of the rec room. "Oh. Hi, Wanda. I went out for dinner with Kevin."

"Kevin's the guy who found you, right?"

"Yes. And, um, my name isn't Jane. It's Annie."

Wanda stared at her. "You mean you've gotten your memory back?"

Annie nodded. "Yes."

"That's wonderful! And the name Annie suits you a lot better than Jane does. So what happened? Did your memory just suddenly come back? Or did something trigger it?"

Suddenly Annie didn't want to be alone. "Why don't you come to my room? I'll tell you all about it."

"I'd love to. Let me just grab a cola first."

When they walked into Annie's room, Wanda's eyes widened. "Boy, this sure looks different."

Annie looked around, seeing the room through Wanda's eyes. Yes, it did look different. The rocking chair was now in a place of honor, and over it was draped a beautiful quilt that had been made by Annie's grandmother Alcott. Several framed photographs of Annie's parents, Aunt Deena, and Emily and her husband now adorned the top of the chest, and Annie's laptop computer and a stack of paperbacks sat on the dresser.

She'd also brought her jewelry box and some of her cosmetics, as well as a good portion of her clothes, and they filled the drawers and the closet. The room finally looked as if she belonged there.

"These are some of the things from my apartment." She gestured to the rocking chair. "Sit down. Make yourself comfortable."

Wanda was a good listener. She didn't interrupt as Annie told her the whole story, from the moment Sam Roscoe walked into the Callahan Construction Company office earlier that day until the moment Kevin had brought Annie home tonight.

"You really like this guy, don't you?" Wanda asked softly when Annie had finished.

"Kevin?"

"Yes."

"I..." Annie sighed. "Yes, I do."

Wanda smiled.

"He almost kissed me tonight," Annie confessed. "But at the last minute I got scared and backed away. Yet I wanted him to kiss me. Does that make sense?" Every time she thought about those few seconds they'd stood so close and how the air between them had seemed charged with unspoken emotions, she felt that same fierce longing. Oh, yes, she'd wanted him to. She'd wanted him to more than she'd wanted anything in a long time.

"It makes a lot of sense," Wanda said.

"It *does?*"

"I think so."

"It doesn't make *any* sense to me."

"Annie, you were in an abusive relationship. It's natural for you to be afraid of intimacy. And that's what a kiss is. Intimacy of the highest order."

"I..." Annie stopped. Wanda was right. Annie instinctively knew it. Jonathan had done a number on her, and now she was screwed up. She hadn't realized it before now because she hadn't had any close relationship with another man since her divorce, so the question hadn't arisen. "What should I do? I know I hurt Kevin's feelings tonight."

"Talk to him. Tell him the truth. That it's going to take you a while, and probably some counseling, before you're ready to have a normal sexual relationship with a man."

"Oh, God. I don't know if I can."

"Sure you can."

Annie sighed. "I'm not even sure he'll call me again."

Wanda smiled. "If he really likes you, he'll call you. And if he doesn't, you call him. That's what I'd do."

Annie smiled. "You're braver than I am, Wanda. I'm a coward."

"You're not a coward. You left Jonathan, didn't you? That was a very brave act."

Annie's smile widened. That *was* a brave act.

"You know, hon, there are regular counseling sessions here for women who have been abused. They hold them on Tuesday and Thursday nights. You should go."

Annie nodded. She *would* go. "Thanks, Wanda."

Wanda smiled. "Anytime. Now, if you're not tired, why don't we go into the rec room? They show old Cary Grant movies on Friday nights. Do you like Cary Grant?''

''What's not to like?'' Annie said.

''Well, c'mon, then,'' Wanda said, jumping up. ''What're we waiting for?''

Chapter Nine

Kevin couldn't get the previous night and that almost kiss out of his mind. All through Scott's game Saturday morning, he was distracted.

Finally Jack, who'd brought Ryan to see his cousin play, said, "Hey, buddy, what's up with you? That's the second time I've asked you a question and you haven't answered."

Kevin blinked. "What? Sorry. I, uh, I've been thinking." He cast about for an explanation that sounded legitimate. "About whether I'm gonna get that job for Bailey Health Care."

Jack grimaced. "Well, hell, if you don't, it's not the end of the world. There'll be other jobs."

"I know, but this one would be a real coup. Think

about it. A six-story office building with the possibility of a whole community built around it given to someone who's just hung out his shingle.''

Jack nodded. "Yeah, it would be great. So when will you know?"

"They're still talking to prospective architects. They probably won't make a decision before June.''

"I'll keep pluggin' for you.''

"Thanks." A few minutes passed, then Kevin said, "What was it you asked me before?''

"I was just wondering what happened to you last night.''

Kevin frowned. "What do you mean?''

"You said you were gonna stop by.''

"Oh, yeah." Belatedly Kevin remembered that his sister had been invited to a shower, and he'd told Jack he'd come over and keep him company while he baby-sat. "Geez, Jack, I'm sorry. I completely forgot.''

Jack gave him a funny look.

Just then Rory, who was sitting in front of them, said, "Scott's coming up to bat.''

Both Kevin and Jack turned their attention to the tall boy they'd come to think of as Keith's son, even though his father was Susan's first husband, Paul. As Scott walked to the plate, Keith, who was one of the coaches for Scott's team, said something to him, and Scott nodded.

Kevin was glad for the distraction, because if Jack had asked him what had happened to make him forget about his promise, he'd have had to tell him the truth, and he wasn't in the mood for any more raised eyebrows or questions. Especially since he was unsure of what he felt for Annie. He knew Jack and the rest of his family meant well. They just wanted him to be happy, but he wished he could be happy or unhappy in private.

Scott assumed his batting stance; the first pitch was a ball.

"Way to watch, Scott," Jack yelled, punching the air with his fist.

"Way to watch!" Ryan echoed. His bright-blue Callahan eyes danced in excitement as he punched the air with his fist in exact imitation of his father.

Kevin grinned. He reached for Ryan and gave him a hug. "You gonna play baseball when you get bigger?"

"Uh-huh. I'm gonna be the *best!*"

"You're already the best in my book, slugger," Kevin said.

Ryan grinned and wriggled out of Kevin's grasp.

The crowd erupted, and Kevin realized he'd missed seeing Scott's swing. The ball arched high, and for a moment it looked like the center fielder was going to get it, but he didn't back up quite far enough, and the ball dropped, giving Scott a base hit, since this kids' league didn't count errors.

The opposing team decided to change pitchers, so the umpire called time while the new pitcher warmed up.

Jack turned back to Kevin. "So what happened last night?"

Kevin thought about making up some kind of story, maybe saying he had fallen asleep. Then he decided what the hell. "I drove Annie into Pollero and afterward we went to dinner." Quickly he explained about Annie's memory coming back.

Jack didn't say anything for a minute. When he did, his eyes were thoughtful. "You're spending a lot of time with that girl."

Anything Kevin said in answer would sound defensive, so he just shrugged and pretended to watch the new pitcher.

"Look," Jack said quietly, "you can tell me this is none of my business—"

"It's none of your business." Now, *dammit.* Why couldn't he have just kept his mouth shut? Now he really *did* sound defensive.

"I could remind you that you thought nothing of sticking your nose into *my* business when Sheila and I were seeing each other," Jack said in amusement.

"That was different."

"How was it different?"

"Because Sheila's my sister. And I knew what a horny bastard *you* were."

"Hey, watch it." But Jack was grinning. Then he sobered. "I know you, too, and I know you're still not over Jill, so all I want to say is, go slow. Be sure you're not just looking for a substitute for her."

Kevin had suddenly had it. "You know, I don't

understand you. First you tell me how I'm supposed to get on with my life. Then, when I *do* start getting on with my life, you start warning me to go slow. I wish you'd make up your damn mind.''

Jack stared at him.

Kevin stared back.

Finally Jack nodded. ''Forget I said anything.'' He turned away.

Kevin knew he'd overreacted, probably because he still felt guilty about last night. But dammit, he was an adult. He could make his own damn decisions. And if he made a mistake, it was *his* mistake and nobody else's. He was sick of people watching his every move and constantly giving him advice he hadn't asked for.

''You were right,'' Jack said beside him. ''This *isn't* any of my business. I'm sorry I butted in.''

Now Kevin felt like a jerk. Jack was his best friend *and* his brother-in-law. He cared. ''Ah, hell, I'm sorry I lost my temper.''

Just then play resumed, and both men turned their attention back to the game. But for the remainder of the game, Kevin kept thinking of what Jack had said. Even though he'd gotten ticked off at Jack's unsolicited advice, he knew his buddy's warning was sound.

Kevin didn't like admitting it, but maybe he *was* just looking for a substitute for Jill. Or maybe he simply liked having someone to take care of. That thought was completely sobering. Maybe Annie even sensed something of that nature, and that was why she'd pulled back last night.

Because he couldn't have been wrong. At first, she'd *wanted* him to kiss her. He hadn't imagined the chemistry between them. A man knew when a woman was attracted to him, and last night Annie had shown all the signs.

And then something had happened to frighten her off. Kevin didn't think it was anything he'd done, but he couldn't be positive. Maybe Annie just wasn't ready. Hell, maybe *he* wasn't ready. Maybe cooling it for a while, like Jack had suggested, was a damn good idea.

By the time the game was over, Kevin had made a reluctant decision. No matter how attracted he might feel to Annie right now, he was going to back off for a while. And when he did see her again, he would make an effort to keep their relationship that of "friends only" until he was sure both of them wanted something more.

When Annie didn't hear from Kevin all week, she didn't know what to think. Surely even though she might have hurt his feelings, he would have gotten over it by now.

Several times she picked up the phone to call him, as Wanda had advised, but each time she replaced the receiver in the cradle without punching in his number. For some reason she just couldn't make the call. What would she say? *I'm sorry I rejected you, but I'm screwed up.* She just couldn't see herself saying that. Not unless he gave some indication that he still wanted to continue their relationship.

She missed talking to him, though. She wanted to tell him all about the counseling session she attended on Tuesday, then again on Thursday. They were a revelation to her, and they made her feel hopeful about the future.

So on Friday morning, when Justine invited her to go to dinner and a movie with Ange and her that evening, saying, "Ange is dying to meet you, and I want you to meet him, too," Annie gratefully said yes.

The evening was more fun than Annie would have imagined, given that she was the dateless third party. She'd been worried that maybe Ange wouldn't be as enthusiastic about having her with them as Justine had indicated, but it was obvious from the moment she was introduced to him that he liked her and she was a welcome addition to their evening.

She liked him, too. He was a big man with a hearty laugh and warm, dark eyes. He instinctively seemed to know the right thing to say.

"Justine's told me so many good things about you, I couldn't wait to meet you." He shook her hand enthusiastically.

"She's said some wonderful things about you, too," Annie said.

He put his arm around Justine. "We have a mutual admiration society."

During dinner at Rosa's—the same Mexican place Kevin had taken her to for dinner the previous week—talk turned to the center and how Annie liked being there.

"I like it a lot," Annie said. "I wasn't sure I would at first, but maybe that had more to do with the fact I was so confused and frightened than with the center itself."

"How long do you think you'll stay there?" This came from Justine.

Annie shrugged. "Actually, I was thinking earlier today that I really should start looking for a place of my own. I know there's a waiting list at the center now, and I'm taking space that could be used by someone who really needs it."

Justine nodded. "What are you going to look for? A house?"

"No, an apartment or a town house." She made a face. "But I have no idea where to look. I guess I should just start with the classified ads."

"If you want company looking, I'm free tomorrow."

"Oh, I can't take up your Saturday, Justine."

"Why not? I haven't got anything else pressing. I'd love to go with you. It'd be fun. There are some new complexes around that I've never seen." She turned to Ange. "You don't mind, do you, hon?"

He shook his head. "You know I don't. I'll be

busy with the landscaping people, anyway.'' He looked at Annie. ''We're having the backyard redone now that we've had the pool put in.''

Justine grinned. ''It's settled, then. Tomorrow we'll go apartment hunting.''

''If you really mean it, that would be great. I was dreading looking on my own,'' Annie admitted.

They decided that Justine should drive, since she knew the town, but she suggested Annie come to her house and leave her car there. ''That way you can meet the girls.''

''I'd love to meet the girls.''

''I have to warn you, though, they're both fascinated with the fact you had amnesia. They think it's *so* romantic.''

Annie rolled her eyes.

''I know,'' Justine said, ''but they're kids. Kids think all kinds of things are romantic.''

''But things that really *are* romantic,'' Ange said, leaning over and kissing his wife's ear, ''they think are embarrassing.''

''Only when they apply to their parents,'' Justine said.

Annie laughed.

That night, as Annie lay in bed, she thought about Justine and Ange and what a great relationship they had. That was what Annie wanted someday. A relationship with a mature man who would respect her and be committed to her without trying to control her. Someone she could respect in turn.

She still hoped Kevin might be that man. But if he wasn't, he wasn't. Only time would tell.

Because that's what she needed. Time.

Time to learn to live on her own, without fear, and without leaning on someone else every time things got rough.

She'd already taken the first step—attending the counseling sessions at the center.

Tomorrow she'd take the next step.

Where the hell had she gone?

Kevin had held off calling Annie all week, and then, when he finally did call her on Friday, they said she'd signed out for the evening. He was so surprised, he didn't leave a message.

Where was she?

Was she on a date?

Because he couldn't stand another night at home with only his thoughts to keep him company, he'd ended up going to Pot O' Gold, where he played a few listless games of darts and resisted all efforts to get him onto the dance floor. Eventually everyone quit trying, and at eleven, he'd gone home.

That was two hours ago.

Kevin got out of bed and opened the French doors that led from his bedroom to the wraparound porch. There was a full moon, and the hills behind his house were bathed in its milky light. He stepped out onto the porch and leaned against the railing.

The moist air—it had rained earlier that evening—was filled with night sounds: the chirping of crickets, the rustle of nocturnal creatures, the lonely hoot of an owl and, in the distance, the faint wail of a siren.

A night that was meant to be shared.

He stood there a long time before going back to bed.

Justine's twins looked exactly the same. Both were tall, slender blondes with blue eyes and pretty smiles. But it was quickly apparent that their personalities were poles apart. Monica was outgoing and lively, the kind of girl who never met a stranger, whereas Melanie was quieter and much more serious about everything. She reminded Annie of the way she used to be when she was a teenager. As a result, she felt an immediate bond with the girl.

"Mom said you had amnesia," Monica said, her eyes alight with curiosity.

Annie had been prepared for the question after Justine's warning the night before. Even so, she didn't like talking about the amnesia because she didn't like remembering the reason for it. "Yes, but it didn't last long."

"It must have—"

"Monica," Melanie said, interrupting her sister, "what about those apartments you were telling me about? You know, the ones Tod Dickerson's dad lives in?"

"Oh, yeah, Monica said. "Mom, you should take

Annie to see those apartments out on Rose Hill. They're really *cool*."

Annie knew Melanie had sensed her discomfort over the amnesia and had deliberately steered her sister onto another subject. What a nice girl, she thought.

"Thanks, sweetie," Justine said. "I'll put them on our list. So what have you two got planned for the day?"

"I'm going over to Becka's house," Monica said. "Her mom's taking us to the mall in Whitley." She grinned at Annie. "Banana Republic is having a *huge* sale."

Justine looked at her other daughter. "What about you, Mel?"

"I'm staying home. I have that French paper due on Monday."

"The landscaping people are coming at ten, you know."

"They won't bother me. And if they do, I'll just go to the library to finish the paper."

"Well," Justine said to Annie, "since everyone's day is settled, I guess we can be on our way."

As they pulled out of the driveway, Justine said she'd done some research and there were really only about four places she'd recommend for Annie. "Two are apartment complexes and two are town house complexes. Oh, five places, I guess, if we also look at those apartments out on Rose Hill that Monica recommended."

"You know the town better than I do," Annie said, "so I'll go by your recommendations."

"Let's look at the apartments first. Then we can have lunch and do the town houses this afternoon. How does that sound?"

"Sounds great."

The three apartment complexes were nice enough, Annie thought, but all of them were big, with more than a hundred units apiece. "I was hoping for something smaller," she admitted.

"You'll probably like the town houses better, then."

Annie did. In fact, she fell in love with the first group they looked at, a small complex with just twenty units in a lovely, park-like setting and surrounded by a high brick wall and coded security gate.

"Sheila lived here before she married Jack," Justine added. "And I believe Keith lived here for a while, too."

The rent on a two-bedroom unit—which was the only one available—was more than Annie had paid in Pollero, but it was still manageable if she budgeted carefully.

"I love it," she told the manager. She was also thrilled that it was empty and she could take possession immediately.

They made short work of signing the lease, which required Annie to pay both the first and last months rent as well as a security deposit of three hundred dollars.

"Do you have any pets?" the manager asked.

"No, but I'd love to get a cat. Do you allow cats?"

"Yes, but if you get one, you'll have to pay a pet deposit."

"How much is that?"

"Two hundred and fifty dollars, which you'll get back if your pet doesn't do any damage."

Annie could think about that for a while. She didn't have to make an immediate decision.

The manager gave Annie a set of keys, told her the code for the front gate, and they shook hands.

By the time she and Justine left, it was after four. Annie was tired but exhilarated. She couldn't wait to move into her new place. In her mind's eye, she was already decorating it. Since the apartment in Pollero had been smaller, she knew she'd need more furniture, but that was okay. She decided she would turn the second bedroom into a combination office/workroom. She'd buy a computer desk for her computer and a bookcase to hold her books and a small table where she could do her craft projects. She smiled. This was going to be fun.

"I think you made a good decision," Justine said. "The location alone is reason enough to live there."

"I know. It's a great location. Thank you so much for taking me out today. I probably never would have known to look there if not for you."

Justine smiled. "It was my pleasure."

When they got back to Justine's house, Annie saw that the landscaping people were still there because their truck was parked out front, just behind Annie's car.

Justine pulled into the driveway and turned off the ignition. Turning to Annie, she said, "Have you got plans for tonight?"

"No. Not really."

"Why don't you stay for dinner, then? We're just going to throw some hamburgers on the grill, but we'd love to have you."

"Aren't you sick of me?"

Justine laughed. "Don't be silly. C'mon. Stay. It'll be fun. After we eat, we'll play Scattegories."

Annie thought about the night at Sheila and Jack's and how they were going to play Scattegories, too. She also remembered how scared and confused she'd been. She felt like a whole different person today. As if her life was finally going to be the way she wanted it to be. "Okay. If you're sure you want me."

They got out and walked up the drive to the back gate. Annie followed Justine through. Several men were working along the back fence, building up flower beds and planting azalea bushes whose buds were beginning to open with deep pink blossoms. They'd already finished one side of the yard, which now boasted a full complement of shrubs and flower beds filled with purple plumbago and yellow and orange lantana.

"It looks beautiful," Annie said.

Justine's smile was pleased. "It does, doesn't it? This outfit came highly recommended, and I can see why. They do good work."

Just then Ange walked out of the house. "Hey, you girls are back." He kissed Justine's cheek. "So how'd you do?"

They talked about the town house Annie had rented, then Justine and Annie left Ange to keep an eye on the landscapers' progress and headed into the house. When they walked into the kitchen, they discovered Melanie and a young, good-looking blond man standing there laughing. He was obviously one of the landscapers, because his shorts and T-shirt were sweaty and dirty. He held a half-filled glass in his hand of something that looked like lemonade.

Justine stopped dead. Melanie flushed as her gaze met her mother's. "Mom," she said. "Hi. I didn't know you were home."

"Hi." Justine looked pointedly at the young man.

"Hello, Mrs. Carlucci," he said. "I'm Brad Northcutt." He grinned. "I'd shake hands, but I'm kind of dirty."

Annie remembered that the name on the truck out front had said Northcutt Landscaping.

"Hello, Brad," Justine said. "You're doing a good job out there."

"Thanks. I'll tell my uncle. He owns the business.'' He turned his gaze back to Melanie. ''Well, thanks for the lemonade, Melanie. I'd better be getting back to work.''

''You're welcome.'' Melanie's eyes were shining.

It was obvious to Annie that Melanie liked Brad Northcutt.

Once he'd left the kitchen, Justine said, ''Did you offer the other men some lemonade, too?''

''I was just getting ready to take some out to them,'' Melanie said, pointing to a tray on the counter behind her.

''How did Mr. Northcutt happen to come in the house, anyway?'' Justine said casually as Melanie picked up the tray.

Melanie shrugged. ''I think Ange invited him in.'' She didn't meet her mother's eyes.

Justine looked at Annie after Melanie took the tray out back. ''I'm glad he's only going to be here a couple of days.''

Annie understood. Brad Northcutt seemed nice, but he was too old for Melanie. He looked as if he were in his midtwenties, maybe even older, and Melanie was only eighteen. ''They *were* just talking,'' she pointed out.

Justine sighed. ''I know, but I worry. Especially about Mel. She's sensitive and too serious.''

''Those are not bad traits.''

''I know.'' Justine sighed again. ''But she's also kind of innocent and idealistic.'' She grimaced. ''Damn. It's hard being a parent. You want to protect them. Keep them from making bad decisions and choices. And you can't. You just have to pray they're sensible enough to keep from totally messing up their lives.''

For the rest of the evening, Annie thought about what Justine had said. She would have given anything to have had a mother like Justine when she was Melanie's age. A mother who cared. Maybe if she had, she wouldn't have made her own bad choice with Jonathan.

Justine is exactly the kind of mother I want to be someday.

When it was time for Annie to leave, the twins echoed Justine and Ange's invitation to come back often.

Melanie even shyly asked if she could call Annie sometime. ''You know, just to talk,'' she said.

Annie was touched. ''Of course. I'd love that.''

As she drove back to the center, she thought how lucky she was to have been found by Kevin. Because of him, she had a job she loved, she'd made a wonderful friend in Justine and now in her family, and she was getting ready to move into a beautiful town house. Even if their friendship didn't last, even if he'd decided she was more trouble than she was worth, that was okay. He would always occupy a special place in her heart.

''Message for you, Annie,'' said the front desk volunteer when she walked into the center. The girl was clearing her desk, obviously getting ready to leave for the night. She handed Annie a pink slip. It said: "Kevin called and wants you to call him." The time on the message was 1:30 p.m.

Annie knew she was grinning like a fool. He'd called! She looked at her watch. It was now ten o'clock. She debated whether or not to call him back now and finally decided it was too late.

She was so relieved. At least now she knew he wasn't mad at her. He'd probably just been really busy this past week. She couldn't wait to talk to him and tell him all about the town house.

If he said he wanted to see her, maybe she would invite him to dinner. That would be fitting, having Kevin as her first guest in her new home.

As she prepared for bed, she decided today had been one of the best days of her life. And God willing, they would only get better.

Chapter Ten

Kevin poured himself a cup of coffee and stood drinking it on the back porch. Today was going to be a nice day. Clear and sunny and not too hot.

He wished he had something special to look forward to today. He was tired of spending Sunday afternoons at his parents' home. Not that he didn't enjoy being with his family. He did. He guessed what he was tired of was being alone. He wanted what Keith and Patrick and Sheila had. Someone of his own.

Wasn't it ironic? Until he'd met Jill, he'd been the most confirmed bachelor anyone could ever find. His main goal in life had been to stay loose and have fun. Now all that had changed.

Annie.

He hadn't been able to stop thinking about her. It was nine days since he'd seen her, and he missed her.

Where had she been Friday night and all day yesterday? He couldn't imagine. It wasn't as if she knew many people in town. Maybe she *had* had a date? That possibility was what had been tormenting him.

He thought about all the guys who worked for his father's company. Many of them were single. A couple were the kind of guy women were attracted to, too. Like Kenny Romero. Jealousy knifed Kevin as he imagined Annie out with Kenny.

Pushing the unwanted image out of his mind, he finished his coffee and walked back into the kitchen. He was pouring himself a second cup and halfheartedly thinking about making French toast for his breakfast when the phone rang. Picking it up, he saw the number of the women's center on the caller ID screen.

Annie!

He grinned and punched the on button. "Hello?"

"Kevin? Hi. It's Annie."

"Hi, Annie."

"I'm sorry I didn't call you back yesterday, but I didn't get your message until ten last night, and I was afraid that might be too late."

Kevin thought about how he'd waited until after eleven to hear from her. "That's okay."

For a long, awkward moment, neither said anything else.

"I called you Friday night, too." He wanted to ask where she'd been, but he couldn't think of a way to do it that wouldn't sound as if he thought he was entitled to know.

"I went out to dinner with Justine and her husband on Friday night."

Relief made him smile. "I thought maybe you had a hot date or something."

"A hot date? *Me?*"

"Don't sound so amazed. Why shouldn't you have a hot date?"

She laughed. "Well, for one thing, I hardly know anyone here. And even if I did, I'm not ready for anything like that. Dating, I mean."

Kevin was glad she couldn't know what he'd been thinking. "What did you do yesterday?" he asked casually.

"Justine took me around to look at apartments."

Kevin was surprised. "Are you ready to move?"

"I think I should. They've got a waiting list here now. I feel bad taking up space."

"So'd you have any luck today?"

"Yes, we found a place."

Kevin listened as she described the town house she'd rented. He could hear how excited she was, and he was glad for her. He was also—selfishly—glad that she'd be out of the center and more accessible.

"I know those town houses," he said when she'd finished. "They're really nice."

"Yes, Justine said Sheila had lived there before she was married. And your brother Keith?"

"Yeah. Keith was there for a while before he and Susan got married. So when are you moving?"

"Next weekend, I hope."

"What do you mean, you hope?"

"Well, I've got to find a mover that'll take the job on such short notice. I got home too late last night to make any calls, and I doubt anyone's open on Sundays."

"You don't need a mover. I'll get a couple of my brothers to help, and we'll move you."

"Kevin, I can't ask you to do that."

"You're not asking. I'm offering."

"No, it's too much."

"It's nothing. I saw what you've got in that apartment. None of it is big or real heavy. It'll be a snap. We can get you moved in a couple of hours. We'll take one of the big trucks from the business. Load everything up in one haul."

She started to protest, but he wouldn't listen, and she finally said okay.

"We don't even have to wait till next weekend to get started," he said. "I can come over this afternoon and load up some of the small stuff."

"Oh, that would be wonderful. But don't you have things to do today? I don't want to take you away from your family."

"I see my family all the time. Tell you what. I'll have some breakfast, then I'll come over to the center and get you. How about eleven o'clock?''

''Perfect. Um, do you know where we can get some boxes? I don't have any.''

''There's a U-Haul place out on the highway. They open at noon on Sundays. We can get anything you need there.'' He thought for a minute. ''Since we need to stop there first, I'd better wait until about 11:45 to pick you up.''

''All right. See you then.''

He was smiling when he hung up the phone. He knew Jack would shake his head and tell him he wasn't being smart. But Kevin was tired of being smart. He was tired of listening to other people, too.

From now on he was going to follow his own instincts. And those instincts were telling him there'd been a reason he was the one to find Annie.

Maybe she *wasn't* ready for anything more than friendship right now. Maybe he wasn't, either. But that didn't mean they couldn't spend time together. That didn't mean they couldn't be friends.

He'd been stupid to stay away from her all week. Because if he wasn't with her, how would he know when they *were* ready for something more?

''See?'' Kevin said. ''I told you it would be a breeze.''

Annie grinned. Kevin had been right. He and his

brothers Glenn and Rory had moved her in less than five hours, start to finish.

Of course, she and Kevin had gone over to the apartment in Pollero several times during the week and moved all of her small stuff, and all that had been left were the bigger pieces of furniture.

"You sure everything's where you want it to be?" he asked, looking around. "I don't mind moving stuff around for you. Just tell me where you want it placed."

"It's all fine where it is." She slowly studied the living room. Her furniture wasn't expensive; most had been bought at a discount place. But that didn't matter. Annie didn't care about having expensive things; money had never been important to her. What mattered was that everything in this room was hers. She'd picked out every piece: every pillow, every painting, every stick of furniture. No one had told her what to do or what not to do.

For the first time in her life, she was the mistress of her own domain. She grinned, reminded of *Seinfeld*, which had been one of her favorite TV shows, long since relegated to reruns on oldie stations.

She'd always been so envious of the characters on the show. They might be neurotic, but at least they were independent, and no one was telling them what to do and what to wear and even what to think, the way Jonathan had for so long. *And whose fault was that?* But she didn't want to beat herself up about Jonathan. Jonathan was finished. He was the past. Today was the beginning of the future, the first day of her new life as an independent woman in Rainbow's End.

Her eye fell on her aunt Deena's rocking chair. It stood in the corner, on one side of the fireplace. "Now all I need is a cat and everything will be perfect," she said.

"A cat?"

She nodded. "Uh-huh. I've always wanted a cat or two, but Jonathan said they were messy."

"Cats aren't messy."

"I know. He just didn't want me to have anything that would take away any time or attention from him." She didn't seem able to get away from thoughts of Jonathan today, she thought ruefully.

Kevin studied her for a moment, his blue eyes thoughtful. "If you really want a cat, it's not too late to get to the animal shelter. They're open until five."

For a moment she was taken aback. She hadn't expected him to seize upon her statement so literally. But it didn't take long for her to realize that was *exactly* what she wanted to do. Getting a cat would be the ultimate statement of independence and the perfect way to begin this wonderful new phase of her life. "I'd *love* to go to the shelter."

He grinned. "Let's go, then."

Twenty minutes later Kevin drove into the parking lot of a small strip center on the northern edge of town. Wedged between Carol's Cut 'n' Curl and a dollar store was the Rainbow's End Animal Shelter, proclaimed in big block lettering on the store-front window.

When they walked into the shelter, the first thing Annie noticed was the smell: disinfectant mixed in with the unmistakable odor of animals. She could hear them, too. From somewhere out of sight dogs barked and cats meowed.

A dark-haired teenage boy sat behind a chest-high counter. He stood when they entered. "Kevin, hi." He grinned and stuck out his hand.

"Hey, Jason." Kevin shook the boy's hand. "I didn't know you worked here."

"Yeah, I've been working weekends since September. Trying to save up money for college."

"That's right. You graduate next month, don't you?"

"Yep."

Turning to Annie, Kevin said, "Annie, this is Jason Tate, my nephew by marriage. My cousin Maggie married his father, who's the local sheriff. Jason, this is Annie Alcott, a friend of mine."

"Hi, Annie. Pleased to meet you."

"Hello, Jason."

"So, Jason," Kevin said, "where're you going to school? UT?"

"Nope. I've been accepted at the University of Houston."

"Really?"

"Yeah. They've got one of the best creative writing programs in the state. That's what I want to study.''

''Where'd you kids get all your creativity?'' Kevin asked. To Annie he added, ''Jason's sister Hannah is going to an art school in New York.''

''That's what Dad keeps wondering,'' Jason said, grinning. ''He can't draw a straight line, and his writing skills…'' Jason made a face. ''Terrible.''

''He's got other talents.''

''I know. So what brings you here today?''

''We came to adopt a cat for Annie.''

''This is a good day to pick out a cat,'' Jason said to Annie. ''Yesterday we got two litters of kittens, plus we've got a whole bunch of older cats. They're harder to place.''

Annie thought she might prefer an older cat, one who was already litter box trained, but kittens were adorable, too. Oh, she was so glad Kevin had suggested coming here.

Jason opened a door to his right and beckoned them to follow. They entered a large room with cages around the perimeter and several cages in the center. All were filled with cats of various ages, sizes and breeds.

''Let's start here, and I'll tell you about them as we go,'' Jason said. He stopped at the first cage on the right, which held two cats, both long-haired. One was gray-and-white with green eyes and one was champagne and dark brown with blue eyes. The champagne cat cowered at the back of the cage, but the gray and white one reached out his paw as if he wanted to touch Annie.

"Oh," Annie said. She was immediately captivated.

"We just got those two this past week," Jason said. "They're litter mates. The gray-and-white is a male, the champagne-colored one is a female. She's got some Siamese in her." He laughed. "You're not gonna believe their names. Precious and Powder Puff."

"Precious and Powder Puff!" Kevin said.

"Yeah." Jason shook his head. "If I was gonna take those two, I'd change their names fast."

Kevin laughed.

"How old are they?" Annie said.

"Six months old."

"They're adorable." The gray-and-white was still trying to touch her. She reached inside the cage and scratched his neck. He immediately started to purr. "How could anyone give up such darling cats?"

"The owners said one of their kids was allergic. They couldn't keep them."

Annie kept petting the gray-and-white. She wished the champagne-colored one would come closer, but she was obviously too shy. She was a beauty. They were both beautiful cats. Annie looked at Kevin. "I think I'm in love."

Kevin smiled. "Don't you want to look at the rest of the cats before making a decision?"

Annie shook her head. "No. I want these two."

Jason grinned. "Great. Let's go get the paperwork done and then they're yours."

Annie had to fill out some forms and sign a paper saying she'd get both cats neutered, then write a check for $60. In return, she was given the cats' tags, a voucher from a local vet for a discount on neutering, certificates showing they'd received their inoculations for the year, a week's supply of food, and a cardboard carrier in which to transport them home. She was so excited she was grinning like a fool.

"Before we leave," Kevin said, "would you mind if I took a look at the dogs?"

"Of course not."

"You thinking of getting a dog?" Jason asked.

Kevin smiled sheepishly. "Yeah."

Fifteen minutes later he was signing his own papers. He'd picked a three-month-old black Lab puppy named Lincoln that looked like a purebred.

"The only reason that dog's here is because the owner didn't have papers for him," Jason said. "And because he just arrived this morning."

They rode home with the puppy—barking like crazy—in a carrier behind the passenger seat of Kevin's truck and the two cats in their carrier on Annie's lap.

"I think we're both crazy," Kevin said halfway back to her town house. But he was smiling.

Annie didn't seem able to *stop* smiling. She couldn't remember the last time she'd felt so happy.

There was a pet store a few blocks from Annie's place, and Kevin pulled in. He waited out in the truck with the animals while she went inside and bought a litter box and litter and a scratching post and some bowls for food and water, then she waited in the truck while he went in to buy the supplies he needed.

Much later, with all the animals fed and sleeping—the puppy on a beach towel in a corner of Annie's kitchen, the cats in the bed Annie had made out of a cardboard box and an old blanket in her utility room—Annie and Kevin were eating grilled cheese sandwiches and tomato soup at her kitchen table and laughing about their impetuous acquisitions.

"So what are you going to name your cats?" Kevin asked.

"I don't know. Any suggestions?"

"How about Bonnie and Clyde?"

"That gray-and-white is too sweet to be a Clyde," Annie said. "What do you think of Romeo and Juliet?"

Kevin made a face. "How about Marc and Cleo?"

Now Annie made a face.

"Popeye and Olive Oyl?"

Annie laughed. "Now you're getting silly."

"I've got it," Kevin said, "Pete and Repeat."

"You know, I actually like the name Pete for the gray." She thought about names for the female, saying them aloud to see how they felt. "Polly. Penny. Phoebe." Suddenly she grinned. "That's it! Pete and Phoebe."

Kevin nodded his head in approval. "That fits. Pete and Phoebe. Those are good names."

Just then the puppy stirred and stretched. Kevin looked over at him and smiled.

"He's a nice dog," Annie said. "Are you going to keep the name Lincoln?"

"I think so. It's a good name."

"Yes, it is. You know, Kevin, I really want to thank you for taking me over there today. If you hadn't jumped on my remark about a cat, I probably would have put off doing anything for months."

"I should thank you. I've been thinking about getting a dog for a couple of years and never did anything about it." His gaze met hers. "You're good for me, Annie."

The clock on the wall ticked, the refrigerator hummed, and in the corner the puppy whimpered in the throes of his puppy dream.

Something stirred deep inside her.

Kevin stood. He walked around to her side of the table. Taking her hand in his, he slowly drew her to her feet. "Annie…" His voice was soft as his eyes searched hers.

Annie swallowed. His eyes were like magnets. She couldn't have looked away if she'd wanted to.

"I want to kiss you," he murmured.

Annie's heart leaped.

"But I won't if you don't want me to."

In answer she leaned toward him and whispered, "I do."

And then she was in his arms. His mouth lowered to hers. At the first touch of his lips, something gave way inside Annie. She closed her eyes and poured heart and soul into returning his kiss.

One kiss became two, two became three. Her head spun. All thought was gone. The only reality for Annie was Kevin. His hands, his mouth, his tongue. The way he made her feel. The way she wanted him.

But when his mouth dropped to her neck, then lower, to the vee of her blouse, and his hands moved up to cup her breasts, Annie suddenly came back to earth, and a feeling akin to panic set in. Abruptly she put her hands on his chest and pushed away. "I—I'm sorry. I can't. Not yet." She couldn't look at him.

"Annie…" He put his hand under her chin.

She still couldn't look at him.

"Annie. C'mon. Look at me."

Slowly she raised her eyes. What she saw in his calmed her. He wasn't angry. He wasn't like Jonathan. Why was she so scared? "I'm sorry," she whispered. "I—I'm just not ready."

"I know, and it's okay. I understand. I'm not going to pressure you." His smile was tender. "I'm a patient man. I just want you to know that I care about you, and when you *are* ready, I'll be waiting."

Chapter Eleven

When you're ready, I'll be waiting.

Over the next month Annie thought about those words a hundred times.

Kevin had been true to his promise. He didn't pressure her. Since that day they'd kissed, they'd been together at least three times a week, sometimes more. They'd gone out to dinner, to the movies, shopping. He'd taken her to two of his nephew Scott's baseball games, and she'd cooked dinner for him at her place a couple of times.

And one night he'd taken her to his house. Annie had been bowled over by the house. Although she'd never thought she liked contemporary homes, feeling they were stark and cold, his wasn't. His home

was beautiful. Maybe the reason for its warmth and
beauty had to do with its setting, surrounded as it
was by hills and trees, but Annie thought the materials used in the house also had a lot to do with
the way it made her feel.

She particularly loved the kitchen. She wondered
why kitchens held such appeal for her. Certainly the
one in the house where she'd spent her childhood
hadn't been very appealing, but then, her mother
hadn't been a kitchen-type person. Annie couldn't
remember any of the meals her mother served them,
probably because they had mostly been restaurant
takeout or something hurriedly thrown together out
of cans or the frozen-food section of the supermar-
ket. Often her dinner had consisted of a cold sandwich and milk.

Kevin's kitchen invited a person to spend time
there. The floor was a rich, burnished dark wood,
and the countertops were a warm, golden flecked
marble. The cabinets echoed the gold tones, and
there was a magnificent stone double-sided fireplace
that was shared by the living area.

Gleaming copper pots hung from a suspended
rack over the island where the huge stovetop and
grill were located. All over the kitchen were interesting details. In one corner a built-in, glass-doored,
corner cupboard, in another an obviously custom-
built, triangle-shaped computer desk. On either side
of the fireplace, wing chairs upholstered in a blue
and gold floral pattern gave the room a homey feel

that should have been incongruous with the ultramodern kitchen, but instead looked charming and a perfect counterpoint to the rest of the furnishings.

And the table! Annie fell in love with it at first sight. It was a huge round pedestal table made of some kind of gray-blue distressed wood. The pedestal was a sculpture of a tree trunk with the branches serving as extra arms of support. The golden-oak chairs sported seat covers made of the same blue and gold fabric on the wing chairs.

"Oh, that table," she said. "It's gorgeous."

Kevin smiled. "Thanks."

"I've never seen anything like it. Where did you get it?"

"It was a special order—designed for this room."

"Really? Well, it's beautiful. I especially love the pedestal."

"Yes."

His voice was so soft she turned to look at him. The expression on his face stabbed at her heart. "Did I say something wrong?" she asked quietly.

"No." His smile had a bittersweet quality. "The girl I was engaged to made that pedestal. She was a sculptor, really talented. She…died in an accident."

Annie didn't know what to say. She didn't know whether to pretend she didn't know about his former fiancée or to admit that Justine had told her some of the story. Deciding the truth was always best, she said, "Justine told me a little about her."

He nodded. "I thought she might have."

"It must have been so hard for you to lose her."

"The hardest thing I've ever had to face."

Seeing the house told Annie a lot about Kevin. She now knew without a doubt he was a very talented architect. She also knew he must have a lot more money than she'd ever imagined, because even taking into account that the house had been built by his family's construction company, the land and materials used had to have cost a great deal. Plus there was a Corvette in the garage, although Kevin admitted he rarely drove it.

"I don't know why I bought it," he said with a wry smile. "I mostly drive my truck."

"Every man has a secret desire for a sports car," Annie said, thinking of Jonathan and his BMW convertible.

One night Kevin said they'd been invited to his cousin Maggie's home for dinner. "You met her stepson, Jason. At the animal shelter."

"Oh, yes," Annie said. "He was a nice kid."

"Very nice. You'll like Zach, his dad, too. And Maggie, of course. She's the best."

Annie *did* like the Tates. Very much. Although Maggie sort of intimidated her. Not that Maggie was snobby or standoffish or anything. It was just that she was so smart and successful—with a literary agency in New York and all—and Annie hadn't accomplished anything in her life.

Maggie and Zach, her husband, seemed to have

such a great relationship, too. Kevin told Annie a little bit about them. How they'd been high school sweethearts and how, after Maggie graduated, she wanted Zach to go to New York with her and he wanted her to stay in Rainbow's End and how that conflict had caused them to break up and Maggie to go off on her own.

Annie thought it was so romantic that Maggie had come back twenty years later and they'd fallen in love all over again. She'd sighed at the end of the story.

"I love when stories turn out right in the end," she said. "I guess I still believe in happily ever after, even though my own romance certainly didn't turn out that way."

"That wasn't your fault."

"I can't blame everything on him, Kevin. Maybe if I'd been different, not such a wimp, things would—"

"Now wait a minute. None of what happened is your fault, and you know it. I don't care what you did or said or didn't do or didn't say. There's no excuse for what that scumbag did to you, and you know it."

Annie sighed. She knew Kevin was right. They'd even talked about this very subject at her last support group session—which she was still attending at the center—but it was hard to change a way of thinking that had been with her her entire life. *Maybe if I'd been a better girl, Daddy wouldn't have died. Maybe if I'd been nicer, Mom would have loved me and she wouldn't have gone away. Maybe if I'd been different, Emily and I would be close, like sisters should be. Maybe if I'd been prettier and smarter, Jonathan wouldn't have beaten me.*

"I don't want to hear you talking like that anymore," Kevin continued. "Okay?"

"Okay."

That night, after Kevin had gone home, she'd lain in bed a long time before falling asleep. She kept thinking about him. How nice he was. How good to her. How considerate. And how much she cared about him.

The past month had been wonderful. At first, after the night they'd kissed, she'd felt awkward around him, but when he hadn't even tried to kiss her again, she'd relaxed.

Right now, life was perfect. She loved her job, her new friends, her cats, her town house—but most of all, she loved living on her own.

She felt *safe,* and she didn't want anything to change. Yet she knew this status quo couldn't last. For one thing, it wouldn't be fair to Kevin to keep him dangling forever. For another, even though the atmosphere between them seemed totally relaxed and easy, under the surface lay a simmering awareness laced with tension. How long could they keep pretending it wasn't there?

Sooner or later something had to change.

Either she had to tell Kevin he was wasting his

time, or she had to overcome her fear and let their relationship go on to the next logical step.

Annie couldn't bear the thought of giving Kevin up. Yet no matter how much she might want to make love with him and see where that led, she was afraid. Making love with Kevin would give him a measure of control over her, and she just didn't know if she could do that again.

And then there was the whole sex thing. The only man she'd ever been with was Jonathan. And sex between them had been disappointing for her, although she'd tried never to let Jonathan suspect. The truth was, she'd never had a climax. She wasn't sure if she could. And that led to another fear. Maybe she was frigid. What if she disappointed Kevin? What if she couldn't satisfy him?

She wished she had someone she could talk to about this, but she was embarrassed by her ignorance and inexperience.

All morning the next day, Annie was preoccupied with the whole matter of sex and Kevin. Justine must have sensed something, because she brought up the subject of Kevin while they were having lunch together, saying, "You're spending a lot of time with Kevin, aren't you?"

Annie nodded. "Yes, I am."

Justine took a bite of her sandwich and gave Annie a sidelong look. "I think he's in love with you."

Annie's breath caught. "You do?"

"Yes, I do." When Annie didn't answer, she added softly, "Are you in love with him?"

Annie took an apple out of her lunch bag and polished it with her napkin. "I don't know. I think I might be."

Justine studied her. "But you're not sure."

"Not completely. I…maybe I'm just scared. I had such a bad marriage. I don't want to make another mistake."

"Kevin's nothing like your ex. He's a good guy. The best, actually."

"I know that. He's wonderful. I just want to be sure we're right for each other."

"Have you told him this?"

"Not in so many words. He knows I haven't been ready, so he hasn't pushed the issue."

Justine nodded and looked out the window. She was silent for so long Annie felt uneasy. "What is it?" she finally said.

Justine looked at her. "I don't want you to take this the wrong way."

"What?"

"I think a lot of both of you. You know that."

"Yes, I do know that."

"But I've known Kevin a lot longer, and…well, he's gone through so much in the past year. I just don't want to see him get hurt again."

Suddenly Annie wanted to be completely truthful with Justine. Gathering her courage, she said, "It's more than just not being sure we're right for each other. There are a lot of things to consider. For one thing, I really like being independent. I never thought I would, but I do.''

''Again, Kevin's not like your ex. He'd never expect you to give up your job or your girlfriends or anything like that. He wouldn't try to control you the way Jonathan did. Guys like that, they're insecure. That's why they have to always call the shots. Kevin is the exact opposite. He's one of the most confident guys I know. I don't think you have to worry on that score.''

''There's something else,'' Annie said in a small voice. I—I'm terrified I won't be able to make him happy.''

''What do you mean? If you really love him, you'll make him happy.''

''I…'' Annie took a deep breath. ''I'm afraid I won't satisfy him sexually. I…oh, God, this is so hard.'' She couldn't meet Justine's eyes. ''Jonathan and I didn't have a good sex life. I've never had a…'' She swallowed and her voice dropped to a whisper. ''A climax.''

''And you think that's your fault?''

''Isn't it?''

''Oh, Annie.'' Justine reached over and squeezed her hand. ''I suppose there could be a medical reason for it, but knowing what your ex was like, I have a feeling the fault was probably his. When a woman doesn't have one, it's usually because the man hasn't spent any time on *her* pleasure because he's

too much in a hurry to achieve *his*. Believe me, I
know what I'm talking about. My first husband was
a pro in that area. In fact, I didn't know what good
sex was until I met Ange.''

''Really?'' Annie was afraid to hope.

''Trust me on this one. If a man is a considerate
lover, if he takes his time and quits thinking about
himself, a woman's pleasure is almost a given.'' She
smiled. ''My advice is, if you love Kevin, take a
chance. But if you have doubts, if you don't think
you want a relationship with him, be straight. Tell
him flat-out.''

For the rest of the day Annie thought about what
Justine had said. She knew her friend was right. It
was time to make a decision.

Kevin was coming over that evening. He'd said
he would bring steaks. Annie had salad fixings and
was planning to buy French bread on the way home.
Maybe she'd buy a bottle of champagne, too.

She was going to take the next step in her new
life.

Kevin wasn't sure how much longer he could
keep his hands off Annie. Each time they were together, it got harder to pretend they were just
friends. And yet, he'd promised her he wouldn't
rush her or put any kind of pressure on her.

So no matter what he was feeling, no matter how
much his body ached, and no matter how many cold

showers he had to take—he couldn't do a thing but wait.

She had to be the one to make the first move.

But it wouldn't hurt to do some subtle things that might help matters along.

He decided that tonight he would bring Annie flowers. She'd once mentioned how much she loved violets and how hard they were to come by.

He picked up the phone. Somewhere in Austin there was a flower shop with violets. All he had to do was find it.

Annie couldn't decide what to wear. Now that she'd decided tonight was going to be the big night, she was feeling all kinds of uncertainties.

Maybe Kevin no longer wanted to make love to her. After all, he hadn't even kissed her since that night. Surely, if he really wanted her, he wouldn't have been able to keep from kissing her again, would he?

What if he had changed his mind but didn't know how to tell her?

What if…

She stopped. *Honestly, what is wrong with you? He told you he wanted you. And he told you he knew you weren't ready, but he would wait. So stop being ridiculous.*

She knew the doubts plaguing her tonight were simply caused by nerves. After all, deciding you were ready to give yourself to someone else wasn't something to be taken lightly.

Take a deep breath. It's going to be okay.

She stared into her closet and finally decided on a soft-yellow sundress and low-heeled brown mules. The sundress had a square neckline with wide straps over the shoulders. It zipped up the back, so if they *did* make love tonight, there wouldn't be any awkward fumbling with buttons. She smiled at the thought. Boy, she'd made a fast transition from being scared to being calculating, hadn't she? But it wasn't really calculating to try to make things go smoothly on the most important night of your life so far, was it? It was just sensible.

At ten minutes to seven, everything was ready. The salad was made and in the refrigerator. The champagne she'd bought was chilling in a bucket of ice. The table in the dining part of her L-shaped living/dining room was set and candles were ready to be lit.

She wished she'd had some fresh flowers for the centerpiece, but she hadn't thought to buy any, so she'd just put one of her azalea plants on the table. Only one lamp had been turned on in the living room, so the dining area was dim and romantic looking.

She'd even found an easy-listening station on the radio, which played softly.

The bedroom was also ready. She'd put on fresh

sheets, lit scented candles and shooed the cats into the utility room and their cat bed.

When Kevin's knock came at the back door, her heart skidded, and she took a deep, hopefully calming breath. Yet when she opened the door, her heart was still beating so hard she was sure he would be able to hear it.

He looked wonderful in an open-necked blue shirt the exact shade of his eyes. He smiled and brought his hand from behind his back. When she saw the bunch of violets he held, she was so touched, tears sprang into her eyes.

His smile faded. "Annie, what is it?"

She was embarrassed by her emotional reaction, but she couldn't seem to get herself under control. Her voice wobbled. "Don't pay any attention to me. I'm an idiot." She took the flowers and buried her face in their velvety purple blossoms. They were so beautiful. It was so incredibly sweet of him to remember how much she loved violets. "Thank you so much. They're just wonderful."

She managed to calm herself somewhat while she searched for a small vase to put the flowers in. Kevin put the wrapped steaks on the counter.

When she turned around, he was looking at her with an odd expression. Her heart, which had slowed, picked up speed again. She didn't seem able to pull her gaze away from his. They stood that way for a long moment.

Then he took a step toward her. "Annie?"

She put the vase down. Wet her lips.

A moment later she was in his arms.

Kevin was thanking all the deities for the instinct that had made him stuff some condoms in his pocket tonight. He hadn't really thought he'd need them, but he had decided it would be stupid not to be prepared. He'd waited too long for Annie to give him the go-ahead. When she was ready, he wanted to be ready.

As he put his arms around her and lowered his mouth to hers, there was only one thought left in his head. He had been given a second chance at happiness, and this time nothing was going to take it away from him.

"Annie," he muttered against her mouth as they came up for air. He wove his hands through her hair and looked down into her eyes. She had amazing eyes. They were so warm and clear. A man could lose himself in her eyes. "Annie," he whispered again. "Are you sure?"

"Yes, I'm sure."

This time when he kissed her, he closed his eyes and let himself feast on the sweet elixir of her mouth, the soft curves of her body, the firmness of her breasts pressed against him and the perfume of her hair.

They stood there in her kitchen and kissed for a long time. And when his need of her had built to the point where it could no longer be denied, he scooped her up into his arms and carried her into her bedroom.

He saw that the bed was turned down invitingly and that the only light in the room was provided by perfumed candles. Knowing that she had planned for what was happening between them made him happier than he'd been in a long time.

"No second thoughts?" he asked as he set her down.

"Not about you," she whispered.

He smiled. "That's all I wanted to hear."

Annie was still frightened, but nothing on earth would have caused her to stop. After tonight Kevin might not want to make love with her again, but that was okay. At least she was taking control of her life, *risking something,* and confronting her fears. Maybe now she might have a chance to overcome them.

She closed her eyes as Kevin drew her close. He kissed her mouth, then let his lips trail down to her neck. All the while he was kissing her, his hands stroked her arms and back. When she felt him tug at the zipper of her sundress, she trembled. As he slid the dress down, she could see their reflection in the mirror on her dresser. She reached for the buttons of his shirt, but her fingers didn't seem to be working properly.

"I'll help," he said softly, covering her hands with his.

Between them, they made short work of his clothing. Her breath caught as she got her first good look at his body, clad only in briefs. He had a wonderful body, with a sculpted chest and arms—testament to all the physical work he'd done over the years—slim waist and hips, and long legs. Her eyes were drawn to the evidence of his desire for her, and for a moment she couldn't breathe.

Although she'd expected to be, she wasn't embarrassed when he studied her the way she'd studied him. Annie knew she had a good body, too. It wasn't model thin or movie-star perfect, but it was trim and curved in the right places and she also knew it looked good in the pale-blue lace bra and panties she'd worn. She only hoped it worked the way it was supposed to tonight and that it didn't disappoint him.

"You're beautiful," he said in a rough voice.

And then he did something that surprised her. He reached out and turned her around so that her back was to him, then he pulled her up against him. Holding her that way, he turned them both until they were facing the mirror. As their gazes met in the mirror, he began to touch her, stroking gently as candlelight danced over their bodies.

It was incredibly erotic to watch what he was doing as her body responded to his touch. He cupped her breasts, then rubbed gently.

"Oh," she breathed.

When his warm mouth dropped to the back of her neck and his hands slipped inside her panties to search and then find the place that had begun to ache with need, she gasped. With his fingers he began to stroke her, and she moaned and stiffened.

"Relax," he whispered, his hand moving in slow circles. "Let me love you."

She bit her lip to keep from crying out. She didn't want him to ever stop, even as she strained toward some unknown crest as his strokes became more urgent.

She could feel his arousal against the small of her back, the heat of his skin and the strength of his arms as he held her firmly against him. She could smell the aftershave he'd used and the distinct man smell that was so different from her own body scent. She could see his tousled head in the mirror as he kissed her neck and ran his tongue over her shoulder. She could also see herself—a woman she didn't know—one who looked wanton and flushed with desire. Every nerve ending radiated with sensation as the excruciating tension inside her reached its zenith.

Her body arched as she fell apart. The most unbelievable sensations assaulted her. And still he stroked and kissed and laved her ear and neck with his tongue, so that the pleasure went on and on and on.

Tears rolled down her face as her body finally spent itself. And only then did he turn her to face him.

"Annie! What's wrong?" His thumbs wiped the

tears away, and she could smell the scent of her arousal on him. "Did I hurt you?"

"No, no..." She could hardly speak. She wrapped her arms around him and buried her face in his chest. She could hear the hard beats of his heart. How to say what he'd done for her? She would never find the words or the courage to put voice to them. "It was wonderful," she whispered.

"Then let's move to the bed, and it'll be even more wonderful."

He kept his promise.

This time when they made love, she touched him, too. She exulted in the sounds he made, the way he kept saying how good that felt, and that, and that. She loved the way he encouraged her and showed her what he wanted. She gloried in the knowledge that she was making him feel as good as he'd made her feel. For the first time in her life, she understood what it meant to be equal partners. To share in an experience that was meaningful to both, where each person was important and valued and trusted.

When he urged her on top of him, she felt triumphant. And then, when they were finally joined, the pleasure was deeper and fuller because it was shared. When it was over and their bodies finally calmed and she lay in the circle of his arms, Annie knew that she had finally found the place she belonged, and the joy that filled her heart could hardly be contained.

"Thank you," she whispered.

He pulled his head back and lifted her chin so he could gaze into her eyes. "*Thank* me? For what?"

"For showing me what making love is all about, but especially for showing me there's nothing wrong with me." She knew he didn't understand, and she wanted him to. He had given her something so wonderful she had to swallow her embarrassment and be brave enough to tell him how much it meant to her. "I didn't think I could…feel this kind of pleasure. I…I never have before, at least not like tonight."

"You mean you've never had a climax until now?"

"No. I never have."

"But why not?"

"Jonathan never…he never touched me like you did. You know…there. He…he just—" She couldn't finish. It was too shaming to say out loud how selfish Jonathan had been, how he'd controlled everything in their lives, and how she'd let him.

For a long time Kevin said nothing. And then he put his hand under her chin again and brought her face to his.

He was smiling. "Well, you sweet thing," he said in an exaggerated sexy drawl, "if you think *that* was great, you ain't seen nothin' yet. Wait'll I show you…" He bent over and finished the sentence in her ear.

Her eyes widened as he detailed what he planned to do to her next.

And then, to her great delight, he followed the words with the deed. He was right.

She *hadn't* seen anything yet.

They never did eat the steaks. Instead, sometime after midnight, totally sated by sex but starving for food, they got up, went out to the kitchen, put the steaks in the refrigerator, and Annie scrambled them some eggs while Kevin made toast and popped the cork on the champagne.

"How'd you know I had something to celebrate tonight?" he said as he poured the champagne.

She smiled.

"In *addition* to this," he said, laughing and pinching her bottom.

"Stop that!" She smacked his hands away.

"Seriously," he said, "I didn't have a chance to tell you, but I got that Bailey Health Care job. They called this morning."

"Kevin!" She was thrilled for him. "That's wonderful."

"Yeah, today's been a pretty incredible day. First the job, then you." He put his hands on her bottom and pulled her close. "I'm not sure which one made me happier."

"Ex*cuse* me?"

He laughed and nuzzled her neck. "There's no comparison, Annie. I wouldn't trade ten Bailey Health Care jobs for what happened tonight."

She closed her eyes. How had she ever gotten so lucky?

Later, when they went back to bed, they slept spoon fashion, and Annie reveled in the feelings of warmth and safety she'd found in his arms. The next morning it felt so good to wake up next to Kevin, with the cats sleeping at the foot of the bed and sunshine streaming through the slats of the blinds.

"Hey," he mumbled when she tried to creep out from under his arms, "where you going?" He tried to pull her close again, but she slipped out of his grasp.

"Let me go," she said, laughing. "I have to pee."

"Come right back. I want to ravish you."

She couldn't stop smiling.

After the ravishment, which was just as fantastic as Annie had imagined it might be, she put on coffee and started mixing batter for pancakes. She wished she had some bacon. Even cholesterol couldn't be bad for her this morning. Nothing could ever be bad again, in fact. It wouldn't dare to be.

She could hear the shower running, and she sighed in contentment. She loved being independent, yes, but it was also awfully nice hearing the man you loved taking a shower.

At the thought, she stopped in midwhisk.

Loved?

Did she love Kevin?

She stared out the window. A male cardinal had

just landed on the windowsill. The bright scarlet of his feathers echoed the bright scarlet of her happiness.

I do love him.

And as if he had heard her thought, Kevin walked into the kitchen, took the whisk out of her hand, set it down and pulled her into his arms. He kissed her nose, then the corner of her mouth.

"Hey," she protested, her heart filled to overflowing. "If we don't eat soon, I'm going to be late for work."

"We'll eat in a minute. I just wanted to tell you how happy you've made me."

She swallowed. "Me, too," she whispered.

"I've got to go to Dallas today. Meetings with the Bailey people. I'm staying overnight. But I'll call you, okay?"

"Okay."

This time when he kissed her, she didn't protest. Who cared if she was late this morning? Who cared about anything but this?

Chapter Twelve

Justine took one look at Annie and broke out in a grin. "Oh, boy. You did the deed, didn't you?"

Annie knew she was blushing. She nodded.

"Well, girl, get yourself some coffee and sit down and tell me everything before Patrick gets here."

So Annie did. Not *everything,* of course. Some things were too private, and she didn't want to share them, not even with Justine. But Justine got the gist of what had happened, and when Annie was finished, she hugged her.

"I'm happy for you, Annie. And for Kevin. He deserves this, and so do you." Her smile was teasing. "So where will you be tonight? Your place or his?"

"Neither. He won't be here tonight. I forgot to tell you. He got the Bailey Health Care job, so he's going to Dallas today for meetings. He probably won't come back until tomorrow."

"He got the job? That's *wonderful!* Wow. What a triumph for him. Patrick told me there were some pretty heavy-duty firms bidding against him, so his design must have really bowled them over."

"He's awfully talented, isn't he?" Annie said, pride ringing in her voice.

"Yes, he is. Patrick told me Kevin always liked to draw, and as a kid he was always building stuff. Of course, the family's business *is* construction, so I'm not sure anyone thought he was any different from his brothers."

"Kevin's the only one to go to college, isn't he?"

"Sheila went for two years. She got an associate degree in business. But none of the brothers seemed to have any desire to do anything other than work in the business." Justine chuckled. "Turns out that's all Sheila wanted to do, too. I guess she really rattled a few cages when she insisted on being allowed to work on one of the crews."

Just then Patrick arrived, then the phone began to ring, so Justine and Annie didn't talk much for the rest of the morning.

During lunch, though, Justine said, "Something happened last night that bothered me. I wanted to see what you think about it."

"Oh. Okay."

"I caught Melanie in a lie."

"Melanie? Really?" Melanie didn't seem like the type of girl who would lie to her parents.

"She told me she was going over to a friend's house to study for her French final. About nine o'clock, our next-door neighbor called. She was desperate for a sitter for Sunday night, and she wanted to know if either Monica or Melanie would sit for her. I knew Monica had plans, she'd told me so earlier, but I wasn't sure about Mel, so I called her friend's house and asked to speak to her. Well, guess what? She wasn't there. The friend—Ellen—tried to cover for her, told me some goofy story about Mel having to run out to get something, but I knew she was lying and I told her so. Ellen finally confessed that Mel hadn't been there at all."

"Did you confront Melanie when she got home?"

"Yes. And she said I misunderstood. That she hadn't said she was going to Ellen's, she'd said she was going to Elena's, but that's not true. She didn't say Elena. She said Ellen Mitchum. Yet I can't *prove* it. I just know what I heard. No matter what I said, she wouldn't back down. She kept insisting I was wrong, that she'd said Elena. Anyway, I don't know what to do. What do you think, Annie?"

Annie was flattered that Justine wanted her advice, but she had no idea what to tell her to do. "If she won't admit she lied, and you can't prove it, there's not much you *can* do. Did you try telling her you knew she wasn't telling you the truth and that you were disappointed because you thought she trusted you enough that the two of you could talk about anything? You know…appeal to her sense of honor?''

Justine nodded. ''That's exactly what I said. It didn't do any good. You know, Annie, this is so unlike Mel. She has never given me one moment's worry….'' Her face twisted. ''Where can she have been? Obviously it was someplace she knows I wouldn't have approved of.''

''I'm afraid you're right.'' For some reason the image of that Brad guy—the one whose uncle owned the landscaping business that had done the work at Justine's house—flashed into Annie's mind. She almost said something about him, then changed her mind. She could be all wrong.

Justine sighed. ''The girls are graduating in just ten days. After this summer they'll pretty much be on their own. It's such a worry.''

''They have to grow up sometime,'' Annie said softly.

''I know. I just pray they don't do anything stupid along the way.''

Annie smiled. ''I'm sure that's every parent's prayer.'' After that the subject of Melanie was dropped, and they finished their lunch and went back to work.

About two o'clock Justine discovered she had left a contract Patrick needed at home. She asked Annie if she'd mind driving over to the house and getting it for her. "Ange is playing in a golf tournament in San Antonio today and tomorrow, or I'd ask him to bring it over."

"I don't mind at all," Annie said.

Fifteen minutes later, armed with Justine's keys, she pulled into Justine's driveway. There was a dark-blue pickup truck parked in front of the house. The back was loaded with lawn and garden equipment, and she wondered whose it was. It always annoyed her when people parked in front of someone else's house instead of the house where they were working.

She walked up to the front door and unlocked it. Once inside, she headed for the study, only stopping when she heard raised voices from the direction of the kitchen.

"I told you last night, Brad, I don't want to see you anymore. Now would you please leave?"

Melanie, Annie thought. That was Melanie talking. Was that Brad Northcutt she was talking to? Obviously, neither of them had heard Annie come into the house.

"No girl tells *me* when it's over," said an angry male voice. "You think you can tease me, then not deliver? Well, babe, that is *not* the way it works."

It *was* Brad Northcutt. Annie recognized his voice.

"Stop it, Brad! Let go of me!"

This was followed by sounds of a scuffle, and Annie rushed into the kitchen. A red-faced Brad

Northcutt was gripping Melanie's arm, and she was struggling to free herself.

"Take your hands off her!" Annie shouted.

Brad and Melanie both turned, and he dropped her arm.

"Annie!" Melanie said, shock and relief warring for dominance in her expression. "Wh-what are you doing here?"

"I came to pick up some papers for your mother." Annie glared at Brad. "I think Melanie asked you to leave."

"Why don't you mind your own business?" he said defiantly.

"Tell you what. Why don't I just give Sheriff Tate a call?" Annie whipped out her cell phone. "We can let *him* decide whose business it is."

Brad gave her a dirty look, then muttered to Melanie, "Fine, I'm going, but I'll be back."

"I don't think so," Annie said. "In fact, if you bother Melanie again, either by calling her or coming here, I'll call the sheriff so fast your head will spin. I happen to know him personally."

Calling her an unprintable name, Brad Northcutt slammed out the door.

Melanie sank down on a kitchen chair and started to cry. "You're gonna tell my mother, aren't you?"

"Don't you think I should?"

"She'll kill me. Please, Annie, don't tell her."

Annie sat down, too. Her voice was gentle. "Look, Melanie, your mom knows something is going on. She was upset enough today to tell me what happened last night and how you lied to her.''

Melanie looked at Annie. She swiped at her cheeks, but the tears kept coming.

''I really don't want to be the one to tell her anything,'' Annie continued, ''but I think *you* should. I think you should confess everything.''

Melanie hung her head. ''I'm so ashamed of myself. I...I was stupid. I thought Brad was so nice.''

''Did he do something last night to convince you otherwise?''

Melanie nodded miserably. ''I was already thinking I didn't want to see him anymore.'' Once again she couldn't meet Annie's eyes. ''I've been sneaking out to see him for a couple of weeks now. He's been pressuring me to have sex with him, and last night he got kind of rough with me. He was furious when I said I didn't want to have sex with him and that I didn't even want to see him anymore.''

''Did he hurt you?''

''No, not really. But he scared me. Still, I thought everything was okay because he dropped me at the corner when I told him to, but then today he showed up at school and followed me home. I didn't know what to do. I shouldn't have let him in the house, I guess, but I felt kind of guilty about the way I'd left him last night. I thought maybe we could just talk and then be friends. That maybe he'd understand. I didn't think he'd actually hurt me.''

''Melanie, don't ever let any man do anything you

don't want him to do, and don't ever let a man make you feel guilty because you're saying no.''

Melanie swallowed.

"I know what I'm talking about. I was married to a man who intimidated me and made me feel guilty. When he…hit me, I actually thought it was my fault. But I've learned better. It's your *right* to say no. It's your *right* to break off the relationship if you want to.''

Melanie's tears had finally stopped. But she looked so forlorn and unhappy, Annie's heart went out to her.

"What do you think?" Annie said, "Are you going to make a clean breast of it with your mother?''

Melanie sighed, then nodded.

Annie smiled. "Good. Now give me a hug. And if Brad bothers you again, you tell Ange or your mom immediately. Okay?''

"Okay.''

They hugged, then Annie got the papers Justine needed and went back to the office.

That night, when Kevin called her, she told him what had happened.

"You should have called Zach right away, Annie. Jesus, that guy could have killed you and Melanie both. You should never have confronted him. How'd you know whether he was violent or not?''

"I could tell he was just a weasel who would back off the minute he was challenged.''

"But what if he *hadn't?*''

"Kevin, nothing happened. I took care of it, and everything's okay now."

"But what if it *hadn't* been?" he insisted. "Don't you think you took a foolish chance?"

Annie was starting to get angry. "No, I don't. I think I acted like a responsible adult, and I thought you'd be proud of me for standing up to him."

Kevin didn't answer for a moment. Then he said, "I'm sorry. I'm probably overreacting, but if anything had happened to you, I'm not sure I could have handled it."

Immediately all the anger drained out of her. "Nothing's going to happen to me," she said softly.

"I can't lose you, Annie. I just found you, and I can't lose you."

Kevin couldn't wait to get home. Unfortunately, he was in such a hurry—and the Corvette was so easy to drive faster than was wise—he ended up getting a speeding ticket just outside of Austin.

"Do you know how fast you were going?" the officer asked.

Kevin grimaced. "Eighty?"

"Try ninety."

"Sorry, Officer. It won't happen again."

"See that it doesn't."

For the rest of the way home, Kevin kept his speed exactly at seventy.

When he arrived at the house, he had several

voice mail messages. The first was from his brother Keith.

''Susan and I are having a family get-together tomorrow night and we're hoping you can make it. Don't eat dinner. We'll feed you.''

Before Kevin called Keith back, he wanted to talk to Annie. He hoped she hadn't made other plans, because this would be a perfect opportunity for her to meet his parents and the others she didn't yet know. And for them to make *their* announcement if everything went as he hoped it would.

The second message was from Rory. ''Hey, Kev, got some news. Call me when you get back.''

The third was from Jack. ''Haven't heard from you in a while. What's going on?''

After listening to the messages, Kevin punched in the code for the construction company office. He smiled when Annie answered.

''Hey, sweet thing, I'm home.''

''Hi. You made it back early.''

''Couldn't wait to see you, that's why.''

Her laugh was soft, and she lowered her voice. ''I'm at work.''

He laughed, too. ''I know. I still can't wait to see you.''

''Neither can I.''

''Listen, my brother is having a party of sorts—just the family, though—at his house tomorrow night, and I'd like you to go with me. Will you?''

''All right, I'd like that. What should I wear?''

"Why is it that the first thing a woman thinks about when she's invited somewhere is what she should wear?"

"Do you expect an answer or was that a rhetorical question?"

He laughed again. "You can't answer it, can you?"

"Sure I can. The reason women always wonder what they should wear is because we want to do the right thing. Men don't care whether they do the right thing or not, that's why they *don't* worry."

"I don't think I'd better comment. I'll just get myself into trouble."

"Wise man."

They talked awhile longer, then Annie said she was going to get fired if she kept wasting time talking to him, even if he *was* the boss's brother.

"Okay, be that way," he said. "But before you go, am I going to see you tonight?"

"Do you want to?"

"I'll kill myself if you say no."

She giggled. "In that case, come over at seven."

"Make it six-thirty and I'll take you to Rosa's for Mexican food."

"It's a date."

Kevin then called Keith to tell him he'd be there tomorrow and that he was bringing Annie. Next he called Rory.

"I've met a girl," Rory said.

"What else is new?" Kevin teased.

"This girl is special. I think she's the one."

"The one? You mean you're *serious* about her?"

"I could be."

"Damn. Wonders will never cease. What's her name? Where'd you meet her?"

"Her name's Rainey. Rainey Kimball. I met her at a party in San Marcos a couple of weeks ago. She's really something. You'll like her."

"So when am I going to meet her?"

"Tomorrow night. That is, if you're going to Keith's."

"I'll be there. In fact, I'm bringing Annie."

"You two are getting pretty serious, aren't you?"

"Yeah. We are." Kevin smiled. He hoped that by this time tomorrow they'd be even more serious, but he wasn't going to tell Rory that. Not until he'd placed the ring he'd bought in Dallas on Annie's finger.

"Guess what else?" Rory said.

"More surprises?"

"Rainey has a twin, and Glenn likes her a lot. He's taken her out a couple of times. Her name's Rachel."

By the time Kevin called Jack, he was wondering what other changes were in store for his family. Maybe Jack was going to announce that Sheila was expecting triplets or something.

But Jack didn't want to talk about anything special, although he did mention that everyone in the family was all agog over Rory bringing a girl to Keith's party.

"I think this is a first," Jack said.

"You're right, it is." Rory had dated dozens of girls over the years, but he'd never brought one to a family get-together. He'd always said when you brought them home to meet the folks, they started thinking in terms of wedding rings.

"And I guess Glenn kind of likes her sister," Kevin said.

"Yeah, Sheila said Glenn called her yesterday." Sheila and Glenn had always been close, since they were the two youngest in the family.

"So what about you?" Jack asked. "Still seeing Annie?"

"I'm serious about her, Jack."

"I thought you might be. Hey, as long as you're sure."

"I've never been more sure of anything in my life."

"How about her? She feel the same way?"

"I think so."

"In that case, I wish you the best."

Annie spent Saturday afternoon volunteering at the center. She had decided when she moved into her town house that she wanted to pay back the people at the center for all the help she'd been given, and working there seemed the best way to accomplish that. So she manned the front desk on Wednesday nights and helped with the children on Saturday afternoons. While she was there, she also continued to attend the support group counseling sessions.

She finished at the center at five and hurried home. Kevin was coming at six-thirty, and she had to shower and press the outfit she was wearing and still have enough time left to get ready.

She needn't have worried. By six-twenty she was dressed and waiting. Kevin had said casual dress, and at first she'd thought she might wear pants, but she changed her mind and chose a sleeveless red cotton dress. After all, she was going to meet Kevin's parents, and she wanted to make a good impression.

She was excited but a little nervous, too. She hoped they liked her.

Kevin arrived at six-thirty on the dot. He was wearing black pants and a black collarless shirt and looked fabulous. Of course, she thought, grinning, she was prejudiced. But he *was* incredibly handsome, and black looked particularly good on him with his black hair and bright-blue eyes. Sometimes she had to pinch herself to make sure she wasn't dreaming that she had managed to attract someone like him.

He was hardly in the door before taking her in his arms. His kiss left her breathless and wanting more.

"You look good enough to eat," he said when he finally released her. Taking her hand, he led her into the living room. "Sit down, Annie."

"Shouldn't we be going? We don't want to be late."

"We don't have to be there until seven-thirty."

"But you said…"

"I know, but I wanted some extra time with you first. There's something I wanted to talk to you about."

Annie sat on the couch and he sat next to her.

He took her left hand, lifted it to his lips, and kissed it. Their eyes met. "When Jill died," he said softly, "I didn't think I'd ever meet anyone again that I could love, but I was wrong."

Annie swallowed.

Placing her hand against his heart, he said, "I love you, Annie. I want to spend the rest of my life with you."

Annie's heart was so full it was hard to speak. "Oh, Kevin. I love you, too. So much. But…"

"What?"

"I…I'm not sure I'm ready to get married again."

"We don't have to get married right away. I can wait. But I don't want to wait too long. Hell, Annie, I'm forty-two years old. I want kids." He stopped. "You *do* want kids, don't you?"

She couldn't help smiling. "Yes, I want children."

He reached into his pocket and pulled out a blue velvet box. "I bought you this. Will you wear it? If you're wearing my ring, I'll feel better about waiting.''

Annie's hands trembled as she took the box.

"Open it," he said softly.

She gasped when she saw the ring inside. It was magnificent. Annie didn't know much about diamonds, but this one, a huge round solitaire set in a platinum band, had to be at least three carats. "Oh, Kevin." She was unable to say more. She didn't move, just stared at the ring.

He took the box from her nerveless fingers, removed the ring and slipped it on her left hand. It was a little too big.

"We'll take it and get it sized Monday," he said.

"I'd better not wear it until we do. I wouldn't want to lose it."

"I want you to wear it tonight. I want us to tell my family we're engaged."

Annie wasn't sure she was ready for a big announcement. She wished they could keep their relationship theirs for just a while longer, but she knew it would hurt Kevin needlessly if she insisted. "Then I'd better wrap some string or tape around it so it'll stay put." She headed for her bedroom. "I'll be right back."

"I'm not going anywhere," Kevin said. "I'm never going anywhere again without you."

Chapter Thirteen

Kevin kept Annie's left hand in his so no one would see the ring until after he'd introduced her to his parents. He was glad Annie knew everyone else by now. Otherwise, she might have felt overwhelmed. Both Susan and Jan had stopped by the office to meet her over the past month, so the only ones she didn't know were Rainey, Rory's new girlfriend, and Kevin's parents.

Luckily, Rainey and Rory were the first people they saw as they entered the living room. Rainey turned out to be a pretty, athletic-looking blonde with a girl-next-door kind of face and sunny smile.

"I'm so *glad* to meet you," Rainey said. She

looked up at Rory. "Your brothers are all just as handsome as you are. It's *amazing!*"

It was obvious to Kevin that Rory was a goner. He had a goofy look on his face and eyes for no one else. Another Callahan brother bites the dust, Kevin thought in affectionate amusement. His hand tightened on Annie's. He knew exactly how Rory felt.

"I like her," Annie said as they moved on in the direction of his parents.

"That's good. She's probably going to be your sister-in-law."

"Really? Rory's serious about her?"

"Hard as it is to believe, I think he's finally hooked."

"Hooked?" she said. "Is that how you feel about falling in love? That you're *hooked?*" She pretended to be insulted. But she had a teasing light in her eyes, and Kevin knew she hadn't taken offense at his use of the word.

By now they'd reached his parents, who were standing by the fireplace talking to Patrick and Jan. They all looked around as Kevin and Annie approached. All four smiled.

"There you are," Patrick said. "Hi, Annie."

"Hi, Patrick. Jan."

"Hello, Annie," Jan said. "It's good to see you again."

"Thank you."

Kevin looked at his parents. "Mom, Dad, I'd like

you to meet Annie. Annie Alcott.'' He grinned, stretching the moment out. ''Soon to be Annie Callahan.''

It took a few seconds for his announcement to register. Then everyone began to talk at once. His mother hugged him, then hugged Annie and told her how happy she was for them both. His father shook his hand, then kissed Annie's cheek and welcomed her to the family. Patrick hugged Annie and congratulated Kevin. Jan had tears in her eyes when she kissed Kevin.

''I'm so happy for you, Kevin. She seems like a wonderful girl.''

By now everyone in the room had congregated around them. The women were hugging Annie and oohing and aahing over her ring.

''I'm so *jealous,*'' Sheila said. ''That ring is a knockout.''

His brothers pumped his hand and pounded his back and made remarks about what a fast worker he was.

Through it all Kevin grinned like a fool.

When the commotion died down, Keith raised his voice so everyone could hear him and said, ''Sorry to steal Kevin's thunder, but Susan and I have something to tell you, too.''

Sheila was standing next to Kevin and Annie. ''Don't tell me you're pregnant, too,'' she said to Susan.

Susan smiled. ''No.'' She reached for Keith's

hand. They looked at each other. "You first," she said.

By now they had everyone's attention.

Keith cleared his throat. "We weren't sure how to tell you this, whether one at a time or all at once. Last week we discussed it with Scott and agreed we'd tell you all at once. That's why we asked you here tonight. We also weren't sure if he should be here, too, but thought it might be easier if he wasn't."

What in the devil was he talking about? Kevin wondered. He could tell by the looks on the faces of the others they hadn't a clue, either. Everyone looked mystified.

"What we have to tell you is also the reason we asked everyone to get baby-sitters and come without the kids," Keith continued. He smiled down at Susan. "Okay. Your turn."

Susan spoke slowly. "You all know that Keith and I met a long time ago, before I married Paul."

"Paul was Susan's first husband," Kevin whispered to Annie. "He's Scott's father."

Annie nodded. "I remember," she whispered back.

"There's no easy way to say this," Susan said. "The truth is, when I married Paul, I was already pregnant with Scott. Paul wasn't his father. He never knew who the father was—I refused to tell him. I told him it was something that happened right after he and I broke up, and the father was out of the picture. Paul asked me to marry him, anyway, and he pretended to everyone, including his own mother, that he had fathered Scott.'' She looked up at Keith. ''Keith is Scott's father.''

If they'd dropped a bomb in the room, it wouldn't have had a more startling effect that her words. Everyone stared at them.

''I won't try to explain how or why it happened,'' Keith said. ''That's something that Susan and I feel is private. I never knew she was pregnant. By the time Susan realized it, I'd gone to Alaska, and she didn't try to contact me.'' He looked at her, and she looked up at him. The look they exchanged was full of love. ''She thought I didn't love her. I left because I *did* love her, but felt so guilty about betraying Paul's trust.''

''Keith didn't find out about Scott until he came back after Paul's death,'' Susan said. ''We made a mutual decision not to tell Scott then. He loved Paul very much, and we thought it might be too traumatic to find out about his real heritage. But Scott's older now, and he and Keith have a wonderful relationship. He loves Keith the same way he loved Paul, so we told him the truth last week. We felt he deserved to know, and I felt Keith deserved to acknowledge his son.'' Her smile was tremulous. ''One other thing you should know—we were encouraged to tell the truth by Paul's mother, Laverne. She's known about Scott's parentage since before Keith and I married.''

It was funny, Kevin thought, but he wasn't really that surprised at their news, and he'd guess no one else was, either. Scott had always seemed more like Keith's son than his stepson. In fact, many people who didn't know about Susan's first marriage had commented over the years on how much Scott looked like Keith.

He wondered what his mother was thinking. She had high standards and was a pretty strict Catholic. Yet she hadn't condemned Sheila and Jack for jumping the gun. So maybe it would be okay. He hoped so. Susan was a good woman, and Keith was crazy about her.

When the talk died down, his mother walked up to Susan and hugged and kissed her. "I've always loved Scott the same way I love all my grandchildren. Knowing he's Keith's doesn't make me love him more, but I'm glad you told us."

"You're not upset with us?" Susan asked.

"Susan, you're human, and so is Keith. Humans make mistakes. It's how you handle those mistakes that count. And you two have acted responsibly and lovingly. It's obvious to me that neither of you ever wanted to hurt anyone else. So how could I be upset?"

On the way home Annie said, "I love your family, Kevin. They're all such good people."

"Thanks. I think they're pretty special, too."

"I can't imagine my mother acting the way your mother acted tonight."

"You mean she would have disapproved of Keith and Susan's disclosure?"

"No, that's not what I mean. I mean my mother just isn't a warm person like your mother is. Like your whole family is. She's sophisticated and worldly, but she's not *motherly*. I can't ever remember her saying she loved me or giving me a hug. She just isn't that kind of person."

Kevin wished he wasn't driving, because he could hear the sadness in Annie's voice, and he wanted to put his arms around her and tell her it didn't matter that her family was so cold, because from now on, she had another family—one that wanted her and would love her just as much as he did.

"Kevin? I want you to go to Boston with me next month to meet my great-aunt. I promised her I'd be there for her birthday. Will you go?"

He smiled. "Of course I'll go. I'm looking forward to it. She sounds like a neat lady."

"She is. And I know she'll be crazy about you." She chuckled. "Aunt Deena will probably flirt with you. She's always loved tall, dark, handsome men."

"Do you think she'll be able to come to our wedding?"

"I don't know. That's one of the things I thought we could do while we're there. Talk to her doctor and see what he thinks about her traveling. She's pretty frail."

Her voice was wistful, and he knew how much

she wanted her great-aunt to be there. "Did she come when you married Jonathan?"

Annie shook her head. "Jonathan wanted to elope, and I went along with him because I always went along with whatever it was he wanted."

That bastard. Kevin wished he could get his hands on him. He'd teach him a much-needed lesson. "Annie, if she can't travel, and you want to get married in Boston, that would be okay with me."

For a moment she didn't say anything. "You'd do that for me? Get married in Boston when all your friends and family are here?"

"Of course, if that's what you want. Hell, I can afford to buy plane tickets for all the Callahans. They'd still be there in force."

She started to cry.

He was glad they had finally reached her town house, because he could park and pull her into his arms. Holding her close, he said, "Don't you know by now that I'd do anything for you?"

A week later Annie and Kevin were in her kitchen making spaghetti for their dinner when Annie discovered she was out of Parmesan cheese. "Darn. I can't believe I didn't put it on the list when I used the last of it. Spaghetti just doesn't taste right without fresh Parmesan."

"I'll run over to Kroger and get some," Kevin said.

"Are you sure you don't mind?"

In answer, he just bent over and kissed her nose. "Hey, it's no big deal. I'll be back in twenty minutes, tops. Need anything else?"

"No, just that."

He kissed her again, this time on the mouth. "Be good while I'm gone."

After he left, Annie stood stirring the sauce and daydreaming. As she did dozens of times every day, she raised her left hand, twisting it back and forth so the diamond on her ring finger would catch the light. She loved the way it sparkled. Loved what it represented and the way it made her feel when she looked at it. Loved knowing that one day in the not-too-distant future, she would be Kevin's wife.

All her doubts about her readiness to marry had disappeared. She'd been silly to worry about it before. Yes, she liked being an independent woman, but Kevin wasn't going to smother her. He wasn't possessive the way Jonathan had been. And he would never try to impose his likes or preferences on her.

In fact, last night he'd said something that had positively blown her away. They'd been talking about his house, and he'd asked her if, after they were married, she wouldn't prefer to have a house that she'd picked out.

"We could sell mine," he'd said. "I've already had a couple of people approach me about it, saying if I ever wanted to sell it, to let them know."

She'd stared at him. "You mean you'd give up

that gorgeous home that you designed if I didn't want to live there?''

''I told you, Annie. I'd do anything for you. Your happiness means more to me than anything in the world.''

She'd thought he could never top his offer to marry her in Boston, if that's what she wanted. But this…why, his house was his pride and joy. She knew how much it meant to him, and she also knew that all his best memories of Jill were tied up in his feelings about the house. It would hurt him to leave it, yet he would do that for her. Give up something that meant so much to him, just so she would be happy.

In that moment she knew she was the luckiest woman in the world. ''I love your house,'' she said softly, ''and the day we move into it, I'll think of it as my house. I'll never want to live anywhere else.''

Remembering how he'd kissed her and how tenderly they'd made love afterward, she sighed. She was so lost in her rosy dream, she jumped when the front doorbell rang.

Now who could that be? Probably somebody selling something, she thought. Maybe she would just ignore them. Then again, it might be one of her neighbors.

Sighing, she turned the gas down under the sauce, put her ladle in the spoon rest, and walked down the short hallway to the front of the house.

Her heart lurched when she saw Jonathan through

the screen door. She stopped, frozen. Oh, God. The door was unlocked. Earlier, she'd gone out to water the hanging baskets and she hadn't latched the door when she came back in. Could she get to the door quickly enough?

"Annie?" He peered in.

She knew he could see her. How had he found her again? She'd been so careful. She hadn't used this address on anything. All her mail went to a post office box in Pollero. Her phone number was unlisted. And Zach Tate had pulled strings so that her car title and registration didn't even show her home address. Yet there was Jonathan. On her doorstep. And the door was unlocked!

"Annie, don't look so scared. I only came to apologize. Can I come in? I promise I won't hurt you."

She finally found her voice. "You've promised the same thing before, Jonathan." She took a couple of steps toward the door, eyeing the latch the whole time. Maybe she could lock the door before he realized it was unlocked.

"I'm ashamed of the way I behaved," Jonathan said. "I'm not going to hurt you. I just want to talk."

Annie closed the distance between her and the door. Just as she reached out to push the lever up, which would lock it, Jonathan reached for the handle. He obviously thought she'd given him permission to come in.

A moment later he was in the hallway.

Trying to keep her fear out of her voice, Annie said, "Come back to the kitchen. I've got spaghetti sauce on the stove, and I need to stir it."

When they got to the kitchen, she walked to the stove and picked up the ladle. The sauce really didn't need stirring again, but it gave her something to do with her hands. She hated that she was so nervous, that Jonathan still had that much power over her. *He's not going to hurt me. It's going to be okay.*

"Annie, I'm sorry about what happened that last time we saw each other. I never meant to hurt you. You know that, don't you?"

She took a deep breath. "But you *did* hurt me, Jonathan. You broke two ribs. And they were afraid I had a concussion."

"But I didn't mean to. You made me so crazy when you said you didn't love me anymore. How could you say that, Annie? You're my wife."

"I'm not your wife, Jonathan. We're divorced."

"You promised to love me forever. Don't you remember those vows? For better or for worse?" He stepped closer. "Stop stirring that sauce, will you? Can't you look at me for a minute?"

She put down the ladle, sighed and turned to face him. "Okay, I'm looking at you. But there's nothing else for us to say. I want you to go. I have company for dinner, and he'll be back any minute."

He reached out, grasping her upper arms. "Please,

Annie, give me another chance. I love you so much. I'll always love you. Tell me you were just trying to punish me when you said you didn't love me anymore. Tell me you'll come back to me.''

Annie was shocked to see tears in his eyes.

''I'm going crazy without you,'' he cried. ''I can't work. I can't sleep. I need you. Can't you forgive me? You never used to be so hard-hearted.''

Oh, God. Why did he always make her feel sorry for him?

''Annie,'' he said raggedly. He bent and tried to kiss her.

She twisted away, and the kiss landed on her cheek. ''I'm sorry, Jonathan. I don't want to hurt you, but it's no good. I don't love you. Now please go.'' She tried not to feel bad about the agony in his eyes.

At that precise moment Kevin opened the back door and walked inside. ''Take your hands off her,'' he said through gritted teeth.

''Who the hell are you?'' Jonathan said.

''Kevin, it's all right,'' Annie said.

''I *said,* take your hands off her!''

Kevin rushed forward, tackling Jonathan and knocking him to the floor. Annie screamed and jumped. She knocked the ladle off the stove, and dots of spaghetti sauce flew everywhere.

Kevin landed on top of Jonathan. Jonathan was kicking and clawing at him, trying to push him off. With a cry of rage, Kevin hit Jonathan in the face.

"See how *you* like being hit!" he shouted. He hit him again.

Jonathan screamed as blood spurted from his nose.

"Kevin! Stop! You're hurting him!"

Annie grabbed at Kevin, but he flung her away and she lost her balance and fell against the table. Kevin continued to pummel Jonathan. Kevin was like a crazy man. He was going to kill Jonathan!

"Stop it! Stop it!" Annie yelled. "He didn't do anything to me. I'm fine. *Look* at me! I'm fine!" She threw herself at Kevin.

Finally Kevin seemed to come to his senses, and he stopped hitting Jonathan, who moaned and held his nose. His mouth was bleeding, too, and it looked as if Kevin had knocked out one of his front teeth. Annie was afraid his right eye was going to be black, as well. It was already starting to swell.

Kevin got up. He had a dazed look on his face. Annie ignored him and reached to help Jonathan up.

"Are you okay?" She grabbed a dish towel to help him stanch his nose bleed.

"I...I think he broke my nose," Jonathan said.

"I hope I did," Kevin said. He'd obviously recovered his composure. "That'll pay you back for breaking her ribs."

Annie turned and glared at Kevin.

"Who *is* he?" Jonathan said.

"The name's Kevin Callahan. Annie's fiancé,"

Kevin said. "And if you don't get out of here in about two seconds flat, I'll break something else."

Jonathan stared at Annie. "You're *engaged* to him?"

Kevin grabbed Jonathan's arm. "Your two seconds are up." Then he shoved Jonathan out the door and went out after him.

Jonathan shouted that he would sue, and Kevin said good, because he'd be happy to face Jonathan in court, where he'd have a few stories to tell about how Jonathan got his kicks beating up women. "Let's see how many patients you have left when I'm done with you," was his last salvo before Annie heard the sound of a car door slam.

When Kevin came back inside, Annie said, "I hope he's okay. You shouldn't have hit him like that. He didn't do anything. We were just talking—"

"Yeah, I see how you were just talking. He was manhandling you, Annie. Why in the *hell* did you let him in? I'm beginning to think you need a keeper!"

Annie couldn't believe it. How dare he assume she let Jonathan in?

"Don't you *ever* let him in the door again," he said before she could think of a retort. "In fact, if he ever shows up again, you're to call Zach. Immediately. Do you hear me?"

"Yes, I hear you. Now you just listen to me. I

have a mind of my own, Kevin. I don't need you to tell me what to do. I can make my own decisions.''

"This is not negotiable, Annie. You are never to let that bastard come within two feet of you again. Do you understand?" Kevin's eyes glittered like two blue marbles and looked just as hard, as he stared at her.

For the first time in her life, Annie felt like hitting someone. Preferably the Neanderthal that Kevin had turned into tonight. Clenching her fists at her sides, she said, "I will not be married to someone who gives me orders like a general in the army. Who doesn't even *listen* to my side of the story. But most of all, I will not be married to a man who uses his fists to settle arguments." So saying, she yanked off her engagement ring and thrust it into his hand.

He looked at her as if she'd lost her mind. "I can't believe you're mad at *me*. I'm the one who loves you and wants to take care of you, and *he's* the one who abused you."

"Don't you understand?" Annie cried. "I don't *want* anyone to take care of me. Yes, I'm grateful you rescued me and helped me out when I was so confused and frightened. But I'm not confused and frightened anymore. I don't need protecting. I can take care of myself. What I want now is a man who will see me as an equal and who will respect me and my opinions and decisions. You obviously aren't that man."

Kevin's face had hardened into an unreadable mask. "I see. And that's all you have to say?"

Annie clamped her mouth shut. Inside, she was a mass of confused emotions and already regretting some of her harsh words. Yet she knew she was right. Kevin shouldn't have attacked Jonathan like that. Not without at least finding out how she was and if he had hurt her. She'd had enough violence in her life. She didn't need more.

Kevin's gaze locked with hers for another long, silent moment. Then without another word he swung on his heel and walked out.

When Annie heard the sound of his truck pulling away, she sank down into a heap on the floor, put her face in her shaking hands and sobbed.

Chapter Fourteen

Kevin was numb.

He couldn't believe what had happened.

But he knew he was right. She had done something really stupid in letting her ex into the house. He could have killed her!

Kevin also knew that unless Annie was willing to try to understand his point of view, they could never have a future together. He wanted the kind of relationship that his parents had, that Patrick and Jan had, that Susan and Keith had. One that would endure and grow. One where the woman was strong and had strong opinions, but where she also deferred to her husband when it came to the safety and well-being of the family. As Annie *should* have deferred to him tonight.

How could she defend that worthless piece of crap that was her ex-husband? It was inconceivable.

Unless she still loved him.

But the moment the thought formed, Kevin knew it was ridiculous. Annie didn't love Jonathan. Yet for some inexplicable reason she still felt some kind of responsibility toward him. Kevin couldn't understand it. Annie was no dummy. She was an intelligent woman, who he thought understood that she was in no way to blame for what her ex had done to her and that she had absolutely no obligation to the man whatsoever.

By the time he reached his house, the ring that was still tightly clenched in his fist had made a deep indentation in his palm, just the way Annie's actions tonight had dented his heart. He stared at the ring for a long time before putting it in his sock drawer, where he buried it from sight.

Annie awoke with a raging headache Monday morning. She hadn't had a good night. It was after three before she'd finally managed to cry herself to sleep, and when the alarm went off at six-thirty, she felt as if a hundred horses' hooves were pounding on her head.

After a shower and two painkillers, she felt only marginally better. Still, no matter how miserable she was, she had to go to work.

Annie hadn't been at the office five minutes before Justine noticed her bare ring finger. "Annie! Where's your ring?"

Annie was disgusted with herself when her eyes filled with tears. "Th-the engagement's off," she whispered.

"What? Why?"

So Annie told Justine the whole miserable story.

"I'm sorry, Annie," Justine said when she was done, "but I think you were wrong. Jonathan is obsessed with you. And it's not a healthy obsession. I agree with Kevin. Your ex is dangerous. Maybe he didn't mean to hurt you before, and maybe he didn't hurt you last night, but after what you've learned at the center, you know that sooner or later, he'll lose it again. If it were me, I sure wouldn't take that kind of chance, and I don't blame Kevin for getting so upset and telling you he didn't want Jonathan anywhere near you again."

Annie bit her lip. "Kevin still didn't have any right to order me around as if I were a child."

"I know, but Kevin's a man, honey. And he was scared. When men are scared, they don't ask. They order. It's their way of taking care of the people they love."

"Well, it scared *me* when he lost it like that. How is he any better than Jonathan if he settles problems with his fists?"

But even as Annie asked the question, she knew Kevin wasn't like Jonathan. He would never hurt her the way Jonathan had. In fact, she couldn't imagine Kevin hurting *anyone* unless he was acting in self-defense or protecting someone he loved.

All that day Annie hoped Kevin would call her. When he didn't, she knew if they were going to patch things up, it was going to be up to her to call him. So the first thing she did when she got home was dial his number.

The phone rang four times, then his voice mail kicked in. "This is Kevin. Leave me a message."

"Kevin," Annie said, "it's me, Annie. I, uh, I'd hoped we could talk. If you get in before eleven or so, will you call?"

Her heart was pounding by the time she hung up. What if he didn't call? What if he didn't want to talk to her?

All night she waited. All night the phone remained silent.

At midnight she finally went to bed.

Kevin spent the evening at Pot O' Gold. Jack kept him company until ten, when he said he had to get going.

"I know, Sheila'll have your head if you're out much later," Kevin said.

"You're just jealous," Jack answered mildly.

Yeah, Kevin thought morosely. He *was* jealous.

"Don't drink any more beer," Jack said as he paid the bartender for the two beers he'd had over the past two hours.

"I won't." Kevin had nursed the same bottle for more than an hour. He hadn't come to the bar to drink. He'd come because he couldn't stand his own company.

At eleven-thirty Big Jim, the owner, said, "I'm closin' up in thirty minutes, Kevin."

Kevin heaved a sigh and got off the bar stool. "Okay, I'm going."

"Drive careful now."

"I will."

Outside, he unlocked his truck and climbed in. He fiddled with the radio until he found his favorite Austin station—one where they played sixties and seventies rock—then pulled out of the parking lot and started the drive home. About halfway there, on the winding, hilly road that skirted the valley and led to his house, he noticed that the car behind him was pretty damn close. Too close, in fact, for a road like this.

"Okay, idiot," he muttered, "if you want to go faster, fine. I don't have a death wish." He slowed down so the car could get around him.

But the guy didn't pass.

Shaking his head, Kevin accelerated to a normal speed. Some people were just idiots, he thought as he approached the last bend in the road before his turnoff.

Just as Kevin turned the wheel to the left, the guy revved his engine and pulled alongside him, forcing him off the road at the steepest part of the hill. Kevin never had a chance. The truck rolled over and over, crashing through a stand of trees before coming to a stop upside down at the bottom of the hill.

Annie came out of the fog of sleep to the sound of the alarm. She reached out, hitting the top of the clock, but the ringing kept on. It was then the digital numbers registered. It was only four o'clock.

That was when she realized it was her phone ringing. She grabbed it. Punched Talk. "Hello?"

"Annie?"

"Yes?" Her heart pounded. Was it Aunt Deena? Had something happened to her great-aunt?

"Annie, it's Patrick."

"Patrick?" she said stupidly.

"Yes. Kevin's had an accident. He's here at Tri-City General. He's in pretty bad shape. I thought you'd want to know."

"Oh, my God! Wh-what happened?"

"We're not sure. He lost control of his truck at the top of Dublin Hill and plunged down into the valley."

Annie was trembling so badly she could hardly talk. "Where in the hospital are you, Patrick?"

"I'm in the surgical waiting area. Kevin's in the operating room right now. He's got internal injuries."

"I'll be there as soon as I can get there." *Please God, please don't let Kevin die. I'll do anything you want me to do, just please don't let Kevin die.*

"Be careful, Annie. We don't need you having an accident, too."

Afterward, Annie didn't remember getting dressed. All she remembered was the frantic forty-minute drive to the hospital and racing in to find Patrick surrounded by the rest of his brothers, Sheila, Jack and his parents.

"Oh, Annie," Sheila said. She opened her arms, and Annie flew into them.

When Annie was calmer, Patrick said, "One of the nurses just called to say that Kevin's surgery went well, and they think he's going to be okay. They're taking him into recovery right now and they said they'd call us when we can see him."

For the next two hours Annie drank coffee and waited with Kevin's family and prayed. No one said anything about her ring being gone, and she wondered if they'd noticed. She wondered if Kevin had told anyone what had happened on Sunday night.

At a few minutes past seven, Zach Tate, dressed in his uniform, walked in with one of his deputies. "How's he doing?" he asked Patrick.

Patrick told him what they knew.

"We know what happened," Zach said. "He was forced off the road by another car. Todd Andrews—you know him, don't you?—had his telescope set up not ten feet from where the accident happened. He was watching for that meteor shower that was supposed to happen at midnight. He saw the whole thing. He gave us the license number of the other car.''

"Forced off the road?'' Patrick said in disbelief. "Who would do a thing like that?''

Zach looked at Annie. He didn't have to say a word, and she knew. Stricken, she whispered, "It was Jonathan, wasn't it?''

Zach nodded. "Yes, I'm afraid so.''

"Oh, God.''

"Jonathan?'' Rose Callahan said. "Who's he?''

It was one of the hardest things Annie had ever had to do, to turn to her and say, "Jonathan is my ex-husband.''

Zach explained that Jonathan had been arrested by the Austin police.

Annie was sick. Kevin had been seriously hurt. He could even have *died,* and it was all her fault. If she hadn't been so pigheaded, so stubborn about doing things her way, none of this would have happened.

"Patrick, Mr. and Mrs. Callahan, everybody, I'm…I'm leaving. There's something I have to do. Tell Kevin I was here, though, will you? And tell him I'll be back later.''

It was nine o'clock before she entered the police substation where Jonathan was being held. Ten before she'd finished telling her story. At ten-thirty she was taken back to Jonathan's holding cell.

"Annie!'' he said, his battered face breaking into a smile.

"I just have one thing to say to you, Jonathan. I've made a full report about the times you beat me. And when your case goes to trial, I'm going to testify against you because I think you need help, and unless you're forced to get it, you never will."

He stared at her. Then, with a look so filled with rage she knew she'd never forget it, he snarled, "You bitch. I should have killed you when I had the chance."

When Annie left the station, she felt as if a huge weight had been lifted from her shoulders. Kevin and Justine had been right all along. Jonathan *was* dangerous. And she was extremely lucky.

She only hoped her luck would continue. That Kevin would forgive her for her role in what had happened. That somehow they could put this all behind them and start anew.

Five hours later Annie sat at Kevin's bedside. He'd been sleeping for most of the day, his mother said. His whole family was still at the hospital, but they had considerately gone outside and left her alone with him, now that it seemed as if he was going to wake up.

He moaned softly.

"Kevin?" Annie said over the lump in her throat. She covered his hand with her own. "It's me, Annie."

It took a few moments before her words seemed

to penetrate. Then he slowly turned his head in her direction. "Annie?" He tried to smile.

"Oh, Kevin." She could feel her eyes welling up. "I'm so sorry," she whispered.

"Wh-what happened?" he said.

Slowly she told him about the accident. He frowned during the telling. "I...I remember the car."

"Oh, Kevin, I was so wrong. I know now that what you did you did because you were so worried about me. I know that your desire to protect me isn't the same as Jonathan's attempts to control me. Can you ever forgive me?"

"There's nothing to forgive," he said. "I love you, and you love me. That's what counts."

"But I was so stupid."

"You weren't stupid. I should never have said that. You made a mistake. I'm sure we'll both make other mistakes, but as long as we remember that we love each other, it'll be okay."

One Year Later

"Emily Rose Callahan, I baptize thee in the name of the Father and of the Son and of the Holy Ghost."

Sheila, who was Emily's godmother, stepped back with Emily, and Jan stepped forward with her twin. Father Riordan, the pastor of Holy Family Church, poured the holy water over the second baby's head.

"Elizabeth Ann Callahan, I baptize thee in the

name of the Father and of the Son and of the Holy Ghost.''

The godfathers, Jack and Patrick, beamed behind their wives. Standing with them were the proud parents, Kevin and Annie Callahan.

The Callahan clan filled several pews. Rory and his new wife, Rainey, were holding hands and smiling misty-eyed at the ceremony taking place. Glenn and his fiancée, Rachel—Rainey's twin—who were planning to marry in just a few months, were equally misty-eyed. Zach Tate sat with his arm around a visibly pregnant Maggie. The pregnancy had been a shock to everyone, especially her, but now she was thrilled about it and so were Zach's three kids. Jan and Patrick's four daughters sat together; each was more of a knockout every day. Keith and Susan, holding hands, sat with their two children. Sheila and Jack's brood, including their newest addition, Jack, Jr., were being tended by Jana, Patrick and Jan's oldest daughter. Maureen Callahan, widow of Sean, Patrick Sr.'s brother, sat next to her daughter. Molly and Jimmy Callahan, Maggie's brother and his wife, were there with their three children.

And of course, Rose and Patrick, who were responsible for the existence of most of the people there, held the place of honor in the very first row.

The only sad note was the absence of Annie's great-aunt Deena, who had died on the same day the twins were born. But Annie chose to believe that Aunt Deena was there in spirit. In fact, each time she looked at the faces of her precious babies, she could see her aunt in their eyes and in their smiles.

"Happy, sweetheart?" Kevin whispered as Father Riordan finished with the rite of baptism and beckoned to them to come forward.

"Never happier," she whispered back, her heart overflowing.

He reached for her hand, and as they turned to receive the priest's special blessing for new parents, Annie was certain no woman in the world had ever been so lucky.

And this was just the beginning. She had the rest of her life to live with Kevin and her babies. And, if their luck held, more babies to come.

"Thank you, God," she whispered, blinking back tears of joy. "Thank you."

* * * * *

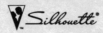

Silhouette®

SPECIAL EDITION™

From *USA TODAY* bestselling author

SHERRYL WOODS

comes the continuation of the heartwarming series

The DEVANEYS

Coming in January 2003
MICHAEL'S DISCOVERY
Silhouette Special Edition #1513

An injury received in the line of duty left ex-navy SEAL
Michael Devaney bitter and withdrawn. But Michael hadn't
counted on beautiful physical therapist Kelly Andrews's healing
powers. Kelly's gentle touch mended his wounds, warmed
his heart and rekindled his belief in the power of love.

Look for more Devaneys coming in July and August 2003,
only from Silhouette Special Edition.

Available at your favorite retail outlet.

Silhouette®

Where love comes alive™

USA TODAY bestselling author

LINDSAY McKENNA

**brings you a brand-new series
featuring Morgan Trayhern and his team!**

WOMAN OF INNOCENCE
(Silhouette Special Edition #1442)

An innocent beauty longing for adventure. A rugged mercenary
sworn to protect her. A romantic adventure like no other!

DESTINY'S WOMAN
(Silhouette Books)

A Native American woman with a wounded heart. A strong, loving
soldier with a sheltering embrace. A love powerful enough to heal…

Available in Feburary!

HER HEALING TOUCH
(Silhouette Special Edition #1519)

A legendary healer. A Special Forces paramedic in need of faith
in love. A passion so strong it could not be denied…

Available in March!

AN HONORABLE WOMAN
(Silhouette Books)

A beautiful pilot with a plan to win back her honor. The man who
stands by her side through and through. The mission that would
take them places no heart should dare go alone…

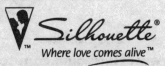

Where love comes alive™

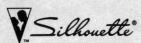

COMING NEXT MONTH

#1519 HER HEALING TOUCH—Lindsay McKenna
Morgan's Mercenaries: Destiny's Women
Angel Paredes, a paramedic in the Peruvian Army, was known for her legendary powers of healing but could not heal her own wounded heart. When she was paired with handsome Special Forces Officer Burke Gifford for a life-threatening mission, she discovered love was the true healer, and that Burke was the only one who could save her....

#1520 COMPLETELY SMITTEN—Susan Mallery
Hometown Heartbreakers
When preacher's daughter and chronic good-girl Haley Foster was all but dumped by her fiancé, she took off on a road trip, determined to change her people-pleasing ways. Kevin Harmon, a reformed bad boy and U.S. Marshal wound up right in the middle of Haley's plans. Was it possible that these two opposites could end up completely smitten?

#1521 A FATHER'S FORTUNE—Shirley Hailstock
Erin Taylor loved children, but she'd long ago given up on having a family of her own—until she hired James "Digger" Clayton to renovate her day-care center. One smile at a time, this brawny builder was reshaping her heart.... Could she convince him to try his hand at happily-ever-after?

#1522 THERE GOES THE BRIDE—Crystal Green
Kane's Crossing
When full-figured ex-beauty queen Daisy Cox left her cheating groom at the altar, Rick Shane piloted her to safety. The love-wary ex-soldier only planned to rescue a damsel-in-distress, never realizing that he might fall for this runaway bride!

#1523 WEDDING OF THE CENTURY—Patricia McLinn
You could say Annette Trevetti and Steve Corbett had a history together. Seven years ago, their wedding was interrupted by Steve's ex-girlfriend—carrying a baby she claimed was his! Annette left town promptly, then returned years later to find Steve a single father to another man's child. Was their love strong enough to overcome their past misunderstanding?

#1524 FAMILY MERGER—Leigh Greenwood
Ron Egan was a high-powered businessman who learned that no amount of money could solve all his problems. For suddenly his sixteen-year-old daughter was pregnant, and in a home for unwed mothers. Kathryn Roper, who ran the home, agreed to help Ron reconnect with his daughter—and maybe make a connection of their own....